SWEET HOLIDAY ROMANCE

A COUNTRY Christmas

COLLECTION

*A Mistletoe Christmas and
A Boarding House Christmas*

DAVALYNN C. SPENCER

CONTENTS

A Mistletoe Christmas

Chapter One 1

Chapter Two 5

Chapter Three 13

Chapter Four 23

Chapter Five 33

Chapter Six 40

Chapter Seven 46

Chapter Eight 55

Chapter Nine 62

Chapter Ten.. 72

Chapter Eleven.. 82

Chapter Twelve.. 93

Chapter Thirteen.. .. .. .105

Chapter Fourteen .. .. .114

Chapter Fifteen . ... .124

Chapter Sixteen . ... .133

Chapter Seventeen 145

A Boarding House Christmas

Chapter One 161

Chapter Two 171

Chapter Three 178

Chapter Four 193

Chapter Five 205

Chapter Six 219

Chapter Seven 228

Chapter Eight 241

Chapter Nine 254

Chapter Ten.. 268

A Mistletoe Christmas

Seek His will in all you do,
And He will show you which path to take.
Proverbs 3:6

Chapter One

Daylight made all the difference.

Georgia Andrews checked her lipstick and hair in the rearview mirror as soon as she slid behind the wheel. Not that she hadn't done the very same thing in the hall before locking the front door. But *he* would be there today and she wanted to look her Sunday best.

Of course, *he* wasn't the He she should be considering. That was God, the One who looked on the heart and not the outward appearance. But God knew her heart was a ball of knots this morning and it took everything she had to hide it behind the appropriate amount of blush and lipstick. Not too much, for then she'd appear clownish and would most definitely draw the wrong kind of attention.

Hence, the need for daylight. Because while the Lord was looking into hearts, *he* looked at how people looked. It was impossible for him not to. Everyone was in clear view from his position behind the pulpit.

Pastor Dave Weatherford *saw* people, which fed Georgia's compulsion to preen and primp.

Good grief, who used words like that?

She shook her head, swinging her hair and temporarily blurring her vision. Historical novelists did, that's who. And she had enough awards on her bookshelves to prove that she knew how to write a good book.

She puffed her bangs from her eyes, an old habit from before-glasses days. Surely there were other old habits that would drive a man her age right out of what mind he had left. Which was one of the things she admired about Pastor Dave—his mind.

It came in a pretty good-looking package too, which didn't hurt.

"Lord, forgive me. I should be praying, not daydreaming about the pastor."

But Georgia had decided quite a while ago—at least two months now—that she would cut herself some slack on that regard. Not be so critical. Give herself a break—however one would say it. Her daughter often insisted she was too self-critical, but Ashton was just placating her. If she knew how lonely her mother was for someone from her own generation with similar beliefs and dreams, she might try to lock Georgia away in a secluded house at the end of a half-mile driveway.

As if that would work.

Georgia took the farthest spot in the church parking lot, considering the walk to the front good exercise. She did the same thing at the market—parked as far away from the automatic glass door as possible. Sometimes she even planted one foot on the shopping cart and pushed off with the other, "riding" it like she used to as a child. Life was too short to miss out on all the fun.

She'd learned that lesson the day her husband died from a stroke.

~

Dave Weatherford wasn't getting any younger, and the younger he wasn't getting, the more he hated the cliché. But it kept pounding him in the ear, especially on Sunday mornings when he wanted to be sly about watching Georgia Andrews try to slip through the door unnoticed.

Trouble was he had to take his hat off in church, so he couldn't be discreet. Didn't matter that the young bucks wore ball caps, do-rags, and everything else indoors. He was a fourth-generation rancher who did what his daddy had taught him.

He glanced toward the back of the church and there she was, silver-streaked hair against her shoulders, looking neither right nor left, nor did she look at him long enough to make eye contact. Politely aloof. Stoic. He had to do something to get her attention for more than a nod and "good morning."

But bumping into her on their way out of the sanctuary an hour later and nearly knocking her down the front steps was not what he'd had in mind.

Chapter Two

"**I** am so sorry!" Dave grabbed Georgia's left elbow and jerked her back up the steps and into his arms.

She sputtered from the surprise assault, and her usual stoicism careened down the concrete. At least it wasn't her.

Gripping his arm with the strength of a steer wrestler, she looked up as if to question his sincerity. Then she let go and lowered her gaze with embarrassment.

She was even more attractive when she blushed. Wait—what was he thinking?

He helped her down to the sidewalk, then released her before he did something stupid like brush her hair out of her eyes.

Get a hold of yourself, man.

"Way to go!" A slap on his shoulder jerked him around to Fred Polk's ruddy grin. "Reel 'em in, Pastor. One way or the other!"

A hard mean streak or else a dry sense of humor ran through these people. They kept reminding

Dave that he was their pastor. Their fill-in preacher. The sooner they got the real deal to take over Red Creek Springs Community Chapel, the better he was gonna like going to church.

~

For the second time that day, Georgia checked her hair in the rearview mirror as soon as she slid behind the wheel. It was worse this time—jostled and wind-blown. Just like the clouds tumbling over the mountains signaling an afternoon storm.

But what did it matter now?

Emotions turned over with the engine as she started her Jeep, backed out, and tried not to hit Rachel Markham's twins when they darted across the parking lot ahead of their grasping mother.

That was what Pastor Dave had done. Grasped her by the left elbow so hard she probably had a bruise.

And if he hadn't?

She glanced in the mirror again, thanking the Lord she hadn't face-planted or broken her nose, and caught him on the church lawn watching her drive away.

She might look a flustered mess to him and everyone else who witnessed her lack of grace, but the Heart-Watcher knew her pulse pounded from more than a near fall. The pastor was the kindest, most attractive man she knew.

At the next intersection, she took a left on Maple and drove two blocks to her cozy condominium. Really, it was a refurbished Victorian split into two apartments. She never heard anything from the young newlyweds next door, and the absence of absolutely every normal sound of living often made her consider switching genres. A cozy mystery plot was settling in her brain like starlings in a stolen nest.

She pulled into the driveway and stopped just short of the detached garage, its wooden door hanging askew on old barn hinges. If she wanted to park inside, she had to get out of her car and set a cinder block in front of the door to keep it from swinging shut. Which was exactly why her white Jeep sat outside, regardless of the weather. In the winter, it blended right in with the snow.

Bible and purse in hand, she headed for the back steps.

Steps.

She maneuvered steps quite well, thank you very much, especially when she wasn't hit from behind. She was not unstable, though *her* steps had a handrail and those at the church did not.

Oh my, pointing that out to the building committee would start a commotion. Poor Pastor Dave.

Her pulse quickened. It must be compassion that enabled him to endure all those committee meetings required to "keep things running." She had narrowly escaped serving on the annual rummage-sale committee herself.

Rummage—another outdated word that refused to die. Ten to one, no one under the age of forty knew what it meant.

The aroma of that morning's peach pie greeted her as she opened the kitchen door. Since her days as a young bride, she'd baked on Sunday mornings, ensuring a homey welcome after church.

Still, after all these years, the smell made her feel safe and accepted. Did Pastor Dave have anyone to do such a thing for him? Everyone knew he was a widower, but perhaps he had a sister or aunt or cousin. Someone to warm his kitchen with the scent of home.

She laid her purse and Bible on the table, recalling how his eyes had lingered on her that morning as he delivered another unpreacherly sermon. His messages often left her applying the day's Scripture to her own life—something the previous pastor had not managed to do.

Before Dave Weatherford took over as interim, Georgia typically sat in the second pew from the back of the sanctuary plotting her next romance novel. Now she sat in the second pew from the back of the sanctuary so she had a good view of him without him having too good a view of her.

But this morning, his dark eyes had looked right into hers as he kept her from falling down the concrete steps. And she had seen fear in them.

A tingly sensation worked up the back of her neck—one she hadn't felt in, well, years.

~

Dave stood in front of the church the following Sunday, welcoming people as they arrived on a perfect October morning. In spite of his griping, he was blessed to pastor this small group. Not that they were perfect. No, they were just like him—imperfection personified. A few would have thrown a couple swear words his way for bumping into them on the steps last week.

But also like him, many pressed into the Lord in spite of the discomfort He caused by rubbing off their rough edges.

From the corner of his eye he caught what he'd been waiting for—the movement of silver-streaked hair against the shoulders of a genteel woman. Thank God, she'd come back. He was afraid she wouldn't after he'd man-handled her. But there she was in a green jacket holding something in her hands.

His heart rate spiked.

"Pastor, you're looking well this morning. Enjoying the fall weather?"

He turned to his right. "Yes, Betty, I sure am. Winter will be here soon enough."

But not Georgia Andrews. She was taking her sweet time getting close enough for him to greet her. Or should he say Daniel Bristow was taking her sweet time, gabbing her ear off?

Lord, forgive me. How inhospitable. I'm here to serve You, not myself.

From the hungry look in Daniel Bristow's eye, he evidently thought Georgia was there to serve him whatever she held in a cloth carryall.

Dave jerked his attention to a somber retiree. "Good morning, Mr. Jeffers. Glad to see you this fine day."

"Hope to hear a good one this time." Jeffers plodded up the steps as if he'd lost all hope.

Georgia and her green jacket broke away from Bristow but stopped at Sophie Hutchins. Clutching her Bible under one arm, Georgia spoke animatedly with the help of her empty hand.

Dave liked that about her. Uninhibited while still reserved.

Forcing his thoughts to the morning's message on being prepared, he went up the steps. In the last year and a half, he'd discovered that his best sermons were those he preached to himself.

Maybe the congregation thought so too, for several of them took notes. Georgia usually did, but not that morning. In fact, she looked ill. Like she'd eaten something he wouldn't feed his dog. A couple of times she fiddled with the cloth-covered item beside her on the pew, then returned her stare to the pulpit, a few feet below his eye level. She didn't look at him once.

Something was wrong.

After the closing song, everyone filed out as usual, but Dave held back. Georgia did too.

He grabbed his hat from the hidden shelf in the pulpit, picked up his Bible, and pushed through an emotional briar patch toward the woman stalling at her pew.

She waited quietly.

His heart sank, but his nose didn't.

She gripped the covered dish like a steering wheel. "I wanted to thank you for saving me—um, helping me—catching me last Sunday."

"My pleasure, Mrs. Andrews." Somehow relieved by her nervousness, he stood a little taller. "It was my fault, you know. I shouldn't have been in such a hurry. Should have been paying better attention."

She held the carryall out to him. "I made this for you as a thank-you gift. I hope you like cherry pie."

And he hoped he wouldn't have a heart attack right there in the aisle before he got a chance at homemade pie from Georgia Andrews. Good Lord, help him.

"Thank you." He took the dish, still warm on the bottom, and his mouth started watering. With his hands full, he couldn't check to see if he was drooling, and he didn't dare lick his lips.

Georgia smiled at last, then turned down the aisle.

"You must have been up early this morning to bake this in time for church."

She faced him, her expression polite. "I bake every Sunday morning. An old habit—filling the kitchen with a welcoming aroma for when I return home after church."

With cherry pie attacking his nose and warmth flooding his hands, his mind was nearly out of reach. "We could share it."

She cocked an eyebrow. "Excuse me?"

"You won't have any pie when you get home, so why don't you come over and share this one with me." He'd never been known for his conversational skills and was beginning to understand why.

"Oh." She pushed her hair behind one ear, then flicked it out again. "I suppose that would be all right. Okay, thank you."

"Just follow me. I drive a white Dodge pickup, and I live out on the edge of town."

"I know—um . . ." She looked around. "All right. I'll follow you. Thank you."

Chapter Three

As soon as Georgia made it to her car, she grabbed her ever-present notepad and scribbled sensations she could use in a book.

With one eye on Pastor Dave as people stopped him on his way to his truck, she wrote:

Throw-up nervous

Obvious

Giddy

Sick

Sixteen

A diesel engine kicked on, and she put the Jeep in reverse.

Was she responding too quickly? Did she appear too eager? Maybe she should delay her departure, but then he'd wait for her, making everything more obvious than it already was. Good grief. She was a grown-up for heaven's sake.

No. Wrong again. Not for heaven's sake, for her own.

She knew exactly where Pastor Dave Weatherford lived. So did every widow and otherwise single woman in the church, but Georgia refused to categorize herself with them. She simply made it her business to know where certain people lived. Fodder for a book, she argued. One could never have too much fodder.

Once he turned off Red Creek Springs Road, he punched it.

Was he trying to ditch her?

Was he having second thoughts about inviting her over?

Reflex kicked in from her early years as a reporter, and she floored the accelerator. She knew what her Jeep could do and would not be out-driven. She glanced at the fuel gauge, thankful she'd filled up the day before.

The flat land slowly gave way to grass-covered hills, and soon they were twisting their way up into cow country. At the second ranch exit, the white Dodge turned off and bounced along a dirt road. By the time they pulled into the yard, her Jeep was taupe-colored.

After parking in front of an actual hitching rail, Georgia glanced at her shoes. Clearly, she hadn't planned to go for a hike this afternoon. She'd be grateful if she made it from her car to the porch without gathering gravel and dirt in her open-toed slip-ons.

Pastor Dave sauntered over in his cowboy hat with the pie in one hand and his Bible under his arm. Before she could take her seatbelt off, he opened her door. "Welcome to the home place."

And offered his hand.

Was he kidding or was he born a hundred and fifty years too late?

Accepting the chivalrous gesture at face value, she put her hand in his, stepped out, then took the pie from him. "We don't want to drop this now, do we?"

His chuckle said he was more at ease than she, and he led the way up broad steps to a wide veranda that she would have wrapped around a Texas-style ranch house. He opened the unlocked front door and stepped aside for her to enter.

"Hang on to that pie and don't let Ruby intimidate you. She has a sweet tooth and thinks she owns the place."

At that, the distant clatter of canine nails on hardwood floor grew more pronounced. Georgia envisioned a massive German shepherd, fangs dripping blood from the last visitor. Instinctively, she gripped the pie plate tighter, planted her feet, and squeezed her eyes shut. There was no rule that said she had to look into the face of her terminator.

A mournful howl opened her eyes in time to see the long ears and short legs of a basset hound slide around the corner at full tilt. Ruby gained her feet just before reaching Georgia's. At least the dog wouldn't be knocking her over for the pie.

"Slow down there, Ruby, and say hello to Miss Georgia."

Miss Georgia. That was a stretch. Maybe he came from the gallant South. At church it had been Mrs. Andrews.

Soulful eyes looked up for a moment, then settled on the pie.

"Nice to meet you, Ruby, but I'm not going to pet you just yet."

Georgia could have sworn she heard the dog's master mumble, "Smart woman."

The airy kitchen caught her by surprise. Windows lined two walls—the west and the north—with unending views of grassland, hills, and mountains beyond. A large table sat before them with no cloth and a clutter of condiments and silverware in the center. Not exactly a woman's touch.

Her heart tightened a bit, and she set the pie on a small island dividing the stove and workspace from the table.

Pastor Dave took two paper plates out of a cupboard and picked up the pie on his way to the table. "Coffee?"

"Yes, that sounds perfect."

As she had baked her pie that morning, he had baked his coffee that morning as well. Of course he would say perked or brewed, but regardless, it was a nice thick cup. While he dug the pie from its resting place with two forks, she used the creamer he'd brought from the refrigerator. Peppermint mocha to the rescue.

Was his disjointed behavior how she appeared in her singleness to others? Doing things she would never have done before? Or forgetting how to do them properly. Maybe it didn't matter after a while, as long as you could eat and sweeten your coffee.

Her heart squeezed a bit more. But it was the look of consternation on his face as he wrestled with the forks that prompted her to interfere.

"Let me." With a smile she hoped was not pity-filled, she took the forks from him and exchanged one for a knife from the table clutter. Lord knew what it had been used for last, but she counted on Him to bless it for them.

"Please, have a seat." As if it were her table and home, she pushed a paper plate to one end, laid one of the forks on it, and did the same for the place next to him.

Next to him.

She would never have been so bold in her twenties, but somehow the years she carried emboldened her. She felt almost entitled—a notion she had once despised.

He dropped into his seat with a sigh. "Thank you."

The mask slipped for a mere blink of a moment, but she recognized fatigue and loneliness. The wish that things were different and the knowledge that they would not be changing soon, if ever.

Oh, those ruthless enemies that clawed at one's soul deep in the night or in an unexpected flash triggered by a familiar word or act so reminiscent of the loved one lost.

A whimper drew her attention to Ruby, who sat by her master's chair watching him with every hope that he would share a piece of whatever was on his plate.

Dave glanced at the hound with affection. "You wait," he said. "You can lick the plate when I'm finished."

Georgia supposed that was all right since the plate was paper. And it wasn't her plate, nor any of her business. Dave could feed his dog in any manner he saw fit.

Dave.

When did he transition from Pastor Dave Weatherford to Pastor Dave to Pastor to— Dave? She forked into what she knew was the best pie anywhere near the Rocky Mountains.

A distant thunderclap rolled off the hills, and the sky grayed with a lowering cloud bank. Here she was, alone in a man's home in her slip-ons and with a storm approaching. Was it a metaphor, such as she used in her novels? Were trouble or danger or sadness about to strike?

A sudden crack shook the house and she jumped, sliding her chair a bit.

Dave reached for her hand, then patted it. "It's all right. Just sounds sharper out here in the country. In a minute it'll start raining, but it won't last long."

Ruby threw her head back with a mournful howl, and rain drops as big as bumble bees splattered against the windows.

~

Georgia Andrews's eyes rounded at the thunder, and Dave's need to protect and comfort her outpaced his good sense. But she didn't pull away when he took her hand. And unless he was a lonely old fool, she leaned toward him a hair. Just a hair.

Two out of three wasn't bad. He was no fool.

Nor was he old. Heck, his father had horsebacked into his late eighties. Dave still rode roundup spring and fall and mended fence and patched roofs, though he hired a farrier. Paying someone else to do what he didn't like anyway made it easier to hold on to what he craved. Someone else could trim and shoe the horses as long as he could be out before sunup, slugging a cup of campfire-brewed coffee and smelling the pinch of hair beneath a hot branding iron.

Georgia eased her hand from his.

He felt the heat in his ears, no doubt lighting them up like Christmas bulbs. "Pardon me. Didn't mean to keep you from eating."

"You didn't, but thank you. I've been watching those giant raindrops." She cut into her pie and looked out the window. "Do you know how beautiful it is out here?"

He'd read her right. She was no feeble female, unsettled by a storm. He followed her gaze. "Sometimes I forget. Until days like today."

She seemed sincere in her assessment, as if she appreciated the land as much as he did. Made him all the more curious about her background. Where she came from, why she lived in Red Creek Springs. Who she'd been married to.

He'd heard the gossip about her widowhood. No doubt he was a similar topic of discussion. Wouldn't tongues flap up a breeze if they knew he and Georgia Andrews were sharing her home-baked pie at his place during a storm?

One of the reasons he lived away from other people.

She rubbed her arms.

"You cold?"

She looked at him as if she didn't understand what he said.

"I'll start a fire. Take the chill off."

"In October?"

"You not from around here?"

She chuckled. "California, originally. But I've been in Colorado long enough to know you can't predict the weather. It just seems early, that's all."

"A fire is quicker than cranking up the furnace. Especially when one of these odd storms hits. It could even snow."

She scoffed, but God must have been watchin' out for him, because a few thin flakes fell, melting as soon as they hit the grass. Laughter replaced doubt. "You *are* good at meteorological prognostication, aren't you?"

He scooted his chair back. "I was a weatherman in my former life."

She followed him to the great room and sat in one of the wingback chairs by the hearth. While he laid a fire, he noticed the way she crossed her ankles. The way her hands rested easy in her lap. She fit in, as if she were no stranger to the house and had lived there for years.

He struck a match. Maybe loneliness was getting the better of him, muddling his thinking.

But when she slipped off her sandals and tucked her feet underneath her in the seat, he knew it wasn't his imagination.

The kindling lit, flames built, and he took a blanket from the other chair and handed it to her. He couldn't wrap it around her because he didn't trust himself not to wrap his arms around her.

Oh Lord, he was in a bad place. A dangerous place.

He went to the kitchen and returned with their coffee cups.

She held the blanket like a shawl, watching the fire, contentment softening her features.

He dropped into the other wingback.

"Clearly, you practice what you preach."

From the angle of their chairs, he had a good view of her expression before she hid it behind the coffee cup. A quick grimace said he should have made fresh coffee. He could drink this thick, old brew all day, but the lady didn't appreciate it.

He swallowed a gulp. "How so?"

Ruby, who didn't appreciate storms, trotted in and dropped at his feet with a snort.

Georgia glanced around the room. "This," she said, nodding at the fireplace first, then at the wood stacked against the wall at one end of the hearth. "You are prepared for the worst blizzard on record, complete with blankets, firewood, and hot coffee."

"And now I've got cherry pie to boot."

She laughed, and the sound warmed the room as well as his insides. It'd been too long since a woman's delight had thawed these old log walls.

God had brought the desire of his heart right into his lonely house.

He looked at the dregs of his coffee. Was it too soon to ask her to marry him?

Chapter Four

Georgia didn't want to leave, but she still had a few wits about her, and when the pie and intolerable coffee were gone, she took her dishes to the kitchen. A sliver of crust stuck to her paper plate, so she set it on the floor in front of the sink. Ruby accommodated her.

Three-quarters of the pie remained in the pan, and she covered it with a clean plate, then folded her carryall to take with her.

"Thanks for coming out. It's not often I have company." Dave had followed her and stood by the stove with his arms crossed as if protecting something. He probably didn't have many visitors, living as he did in the far-off hinterlands. "Oh, and thanks for the pie." He glanced at the covered plate on the island. "I'll return your pan."

She couldn't resist. "And I'm sure you know the rule about returning dishes."

He stared. Swallowed. Looked past her out the window searching for the answer.

"You can't return the dish empty." Since when had she become a teasing flirt? She needed to leave immediately, if not sooner.

She patted Ruby's ear-dragging head, then found her purse and her way to the front door.

Of course Dave beat her there and opened it. An odd spark danced in his dark eyes.

What was he thinking? Had she forgotten to put her shoes on? Looking down, she saw the blanket that she had clutched about her like a memory. Good grief.

"Oh!" Whipping it off, she quickly rolled it into a fat donut and offered it to him. "Thank you for your kind hospitality."

"For a minute there, I thought you were going to take this and be forced to bring it back with something inside."

His merry mockery sent heat flashing up her neck and into her hairline. She gave a curt nod and carefully crossed wet gravel to her Jeep. At least the rain—and snow—had stopped.

But Dave was as bad as Ruby, dogging her steps so he could open her car door.

"You're welcome any time, Georgia. And thank you for coming out today."

Her name had made the same metamorphosis as his. They were suddenly interacting on a first-name basis, though she hadn't said his aloud.

"You are most welcome. The pleasure was m—" A quick cough muffled her mindless auto-response. She wasn't quite ready to reveal her pleasure to anyone, particularly to her pastor who had occupied entirely too much of her imagination and proved to be a warm and hospitable host whose home she didn't want to leave.

When she arrived at her own, evidence of the passing storm puddled in her driveway and glittered on marigolds and mums crowding her back steps. The rich fall colors had taken over her purple petunias. Lavender lilacs and their luscious perfume were long gone, but sunflower soldiers bravely guarded her fence.

Fall flowers would be a lovely addition to Pastor Dave's front porch.

She welcomed the idea without hesitation or embarrassment. "I should have kept the blanket," she said as she unlocked the back door. "I could have wrapped a pot of russet mums in it and given it to him."

There was something about age that defied decorum, that allowed one to look at what mattered in life and gave one the confidence to pursue it. She lifted her chin.

The kitchen still smelled of freshly baked cherry pie, even this late in the day, but she'd had her dessert first. Her father used to say, "Eat the best first and you'll have the best left." When she'd asked as a child what he meant, he added, "Because it's the best you've got."

She hung her purse on the antique hall tree by the front door and looked in the beveled mirror. "Perhaps I'm in the dessert stage of life, because this is the best I have."

The thought brightened her considerably, and she took leftover baked chicken from the refrigerator and chopped it into a green salad. Hopefully Dave had something substantial to eat too, though she doubted it. Fast and easy probably overrode homemade and healthy. He was a single man, after all, and that variety tended to not cook for themselves. Cliché, yes, but one that her readers clearly understood and accepted in her books, proving that some women still wanted to comfort and care for their men.

"Ha!" Their men. She had no men in her life other than her son-in-law, and though he was a sweetheart, he didn't count. Wrong generation.

"Ha!" The sharp note echoed from her office.

"Oh, be quiet, Jack."

That bird had the hearing of a barn owl. He picked up the oddest phrases at the oddest times, and she didn't need the both of them reminding her that she had no man other than the heroes in her novels.

And speaking of her son-in-law, what would her daughter think of her visit to the pastor's house today?

Georgia wasn't about to tell her. At least not yet. She wasn't about to tell anyone else either, not even her closest friend, Sue Vance. What if nothing came of it? What if she never heard from Dave again, other than a polite "good morning" on Sundays or a nervous cough as they passed each other in the center aisle.

How awkward.

"Oh Lord, what have I done?" She had to shove Dave back into his pastoral position. Keep him at arm's length emotionally, and forget she'd been so informal and relaxed as to kick off her shoes and curl up beneath a blanket by his fireplace.

After loading the dishwasher, she went upstairs and changed into her Sunday-slouchy clothes. Another habit from so many years alone. With no one to please, she dressed exactly as *she* pleased. Her rationale stumbled.

Shouldn't one have the freedom to dress as one pleased regardless? Most young women today would insist upon it, but Georgia remembered wearing a certain dress or a particular color because she knew her husband liked it. And Jeff had often worn the tie she had given him one Father's Day because she believed it complimented his blue eyes. Acts of love that only lovers recognize.

Tugging on her oversized UNC sweatshirt, she trotted downstairs to the back porch, where she dug through the chest freezer. Surely she had something tucked away that could be thawed and freshened into a good meal for a solitary soul. The bald belly of a frozen chicken nested between bags of peas and carrots and chopped broccoli.

Perfect. Chicken pot pie. Simple and straightforward. Cook the chicken, make gravy and a pie crust, and serve it in her favorite cobalt deep-dish casserole.

She'd leave it on Dave's—the pastor's—pickup seat next Sunday after church started.

~

Dave cut another wedge of pie and topped it with a scoop of vanilla ice cream so crusty and yellow from being in the freezer that he scooped it right off and into the trash.

Then he made a pot of fresh coffee.

Comfort in hand, he returned to the fireplace chair and settled in. Not enough light in the room, he decided for the hundredth time. More lamps? A new light fixture?

He'd mangled the pie again, trying to get it out of the pan. Hadn't had that problem in a while because before today, he ate his pie and prefabbed meals right out of the dish they came in. Fewer to wash that way.

What would Georgia Andrews think of that?

He scoffed and shoved in another bite of her sweet cherries. Had to be homemade crust.

Valerie had always bought bakery pies, bless her. She loved him and he loved her, but she didn't cook much. More of a survivalist in the kitchen, though he never would have told her that. Made him feel guilty to think it now.

Singleness had crept up on him like a cougar. It had been two years since he'd shared pie with his Val. Not that long, but long enough to know he didn't like it. They used to eat outside on the deck in the summer, in the kitchen watching snowfall in the winter, and in front of the fireplace in the spring and fall.

Would he ever share that with anyone else like he had today?

"I enjoyed it, Lord. As much as You know I love my Val and always will, I liked having Georgia here, eating with her, watching her wince at my coffee." He chuckled. Cowboy coffee, Val had called it.

A knot tightened in his throat, and he had a hard time getting the last mouthful of cherries down. It wasn't that he *had* to be alone. A couple of widows from the church had made a point of inviting his attention when he took on the interim position. But he wasn't looking for someone to take his wife's place.

And then he'd seen Georgia. Nothing like the others, nothing like his Valerie. But she drew him like a horse to clear water.

He tossed his paper plate on the dying fire and went to his study. In the top desk drawer on the right, he found the church directory listing the names and phone numbers of most of the congregation. The church didn't have a formal membership roster, just a list of people willing to share the load, help out when needed, pray when asked.

Georgia's name and number appeared near the top of the first page: *Andrews, Georgia*. He'd expected to see it. She struck him as the kind of woman who would share, help, and pray.

Her number burned onto his retina, and he returned the booklet to his desk drawer. Now what?

Should he call her? Ask if he could take her for coffee one day this week?

The Red Creek Springs Community Church didn't hold mid-week services, and he didn't think he could wait seven days to see Georgia Andrews.

But what if she didn't feel the same?

What if she gave him some excuse about being busy with whatever?

He had to accept the fact that today could have been a one-and-done deal. She might not be interested in him. And he might have to put on a stone face when he passed her in the aisle at church or shook her hand on her way out after Sunday-morning service.

If she'd even shake his hand. She might sneak out the back. She might stop coming.

He grabbed his work hat and set out for the barn with his short-legged hound at his heels. He didn't work on Sunday other than to feed the stalled livestock. Some considered that old-fashioned, but he'd learned that the Lord knew what He was doing when He told His people to take a day off.

Rest was highly underrated in these modern times. An unsought treasure, to Dave's way of thinking. But rest was something he couldn't do now that Georgia Andrews had been in his home with her gentle confidence and sweet laughter.

Ruby curled up against the hay stack for a long nap on a short afternoon. No trouble resting for that hound.

A few paces on, Buddy nickered from his stall, his dark head over the door. The gelding's neck was warm from standing outside in his run. He'd heard Dave coming, as if he knew they'd be leaving. How did animals always know?

Dave led the horse out, brushed and saddled him, then headed north. Once they left the last cross fence behind, Dave kicked into an easy lope toward the first ridge of low hills. From there he'd be able to see the whole ranch and a low patch in the distance known as Red Creek Springs.

Sunlight burned a hole in the clouds, and it glinted like a beacon off the church steeple. The metaphor wasn't lost on him. How could he draw more people to the church? Out of eight hundred in the community, only a couple dozen attended. But he refused to put on a show just to grow the congregation. Entertainment wasn't his business—cows and souls were.

Lately, he'd been giving it some thought and prayer, and the idea of a men's group had come to him. Maybe he could reach a few more with a weekly breakfast group in the back room at the café.

Scanning the huddled buildings, he wondered which one sheltered the woman who, in a couple of hours, had reminded him what home felt like. He wanted to run his idea for a men's group past her, see what she thought about it. See what she thought about him.

What she thought about *them*.

Chapter Five

Monday morning, Georgia pulled her hair into a ponytail on her way to the kitchen for a fresh cup of coffee. The cookie jar lured her off course before she returned to her desk chair with a vengeance. She had a deadline to meet, and the words were holding out on her.

"Lord, please, I need some help here. My concentration is shot."

A trellis outside her office window held a climbing rose that brought to mind a lattice-topped cherry pie. As the pie sharpened into focus, so did a picturesque setting in the country with cattle and horses and cowboys and—good grief!

She pulled the band holding her hair and scrubbed her scalp. She never had worn her hair up successfully. It gave her a headache. Now it was giving her visions of a certain man and his home. She refused to make Dave Weatherford into a character.

"Write, write, write," Jack scolded from his cage across the room, bobbing his blue head.

"That's enough out of you." Georgia glanced at the budgie puckering up to the mirror in his cage. "Don't kiss that bird, he'll bite you."

She was immediately rewarded with a gravely, "Don't kiss that bird, he'll bite you."

Of course beaks didn't pucker, but Jack did his budgie best.

"Jesus, Jesus, Jesus," bounced across the room.

Was the bird swearing? Georgia never knew for sure. Maybe he was simply repeating what he heard most frequently in her panicked pleas.

"Go right ahead, Jack. I need all the prayer I can get."

Jack was not exactly the town gossip, but he kept her company in a one-sided sort of way. A bird of few words, like someone else she knew.

Only recently had she discovered that the someone didn't rattle on with small talk when picturesque silence worked just as well. Was it only yesterday that she sat before wall-size windows in a kitchen nook and later in front of a massive stone fireplace? Had she really snuggled in a blanket so gallantly brought to her by a dark-eyed man with a permanent hat indentation in his brown hair? Throw in cowboy boots and graying temples, and he could be the cover art for her next book.

Her imagination threatened mutiny. She'd spent entirely too much time daydreaming about Dave Weatherford. His words were indeed few unless he was behind the pulpit. However, even there they were well chosen, not selected to impress but to empower.

Georgia's fingers stilled on the keys as her gaze fixed on the trailing pink rose. Her livelihood depended on carefully selected words, but lately they'd been running amuck. She pulled her hair up again, this time into a messy bun.

It was so warm for October, much warmer than it had been yesterday during the sudden downpour and scattered snowflakes. As if complaining about the weather made one snap of difference in a micro-climate such as the Front Range controlled by whimsical weather patterns.

"What a waste of energy."

Her current work-in-progress glared from her computer screen, more white space than black words. The hero was giving her fits, not cooperating with the plot, and running off and doing things on his own. Maybe she should just go along with him and see what happened. The heroine in one of her early books had been just as independent and headstrong, and Georgia had followed her into a frightening wildland fire, the near death of her dog, and high rankings in book sales.

She hated to admit it, but her character had been right.

"Okay, what's on your mind for this next scene?"

Her phone rang.

"Nope, no phones. This is historical fiction—wait." She reached for her cell phone but it wasn't in its usual place. "Shoot. No—don't shoot yet."

"Don't shoot!" Jack said.

Hurrying through the kitchen and down the hall, she checked all the usual places and finally found her phone recharging on a small table by the stairs. The caller had disconnected. No voicemail indicator.

She waited. Sometimes it took a minute.

 The dot blinked on and her heart blinked as well.

The phone was at 92 percent, so she unplugged it and checked the voicemail. An unknown caller.

What were the chances?

"He's not going to call you. Get a grip. This is not one of your romance novels. He's a busy man." Forcing her feet to a reasonable pace, she returned to her desk and pressed a shaky finger to the voicemail icon.

Silence.

Figured.

"Hello. Georgia."

Her name in his voice. She shivered.

"This is Dave Weatherford, uh, Pastor Dave. I hope I'm not disturbing you."

Silence.

She looked at her phone, still populating the message text, and then put it on speaker.

"I was wondering if you'd like to meet for coffee one morning this week. If you're a morning person. At the café."

Silence.

She shook the phone as if that would help.

"Half past eight on Wednesday. Give me a call and let me know. Or not. Or you could text."

A long pause.

This was the kind of tension she needed in her book.

"Thanks."

The recording ended.

She laid the phone face down and pounded out two thousand words on her computer in record time.

~

Dave set his phone on the table and attended to his hard-cooked eggs that had started out as over-easy. Two maple-flavored sausage links resembled charred logs. "Timing. It's all about timing."

He flipped the sausages onto a paper plate for Ruby and considered it God's grace that Georgia Andrews hadn't answered her phone. Voicemail eased the pressure and gave him time to regroup. Or look like he didn't know what he was doing.

It shouldn't be this hard, asking to meet a woman for coffee.

He opened two packets of maple-and-brown-sugar instant oatmeal, dumped their contents into a bowl with milk, and punched the microwave for a minute.

He'd had coffee with nearly everyone he knew and then some. But this was different. Almost like dating.

He answered the microwave ding, stirred the oatmeal, and punched in another minute.

Dating. He hadn't done that in more years than he cared to count and he sure as heck didn't count coffee as dating.

"Wurf." Ruby licked her droopy jowls.

"That's it, girl. Your regular food is on the porch."

He'd never thought dogs could give the stink-eye, but he was beginning to wonder about Ruby.

She barked, and a loud knock rattled the back door before boots stomped in and scuffed the inside rug. "You up?"

More stomping and Justin clattered into the kitchen, spurs singing.

"You gouge the floor and your mother will haunt you."

Justin chucked a laugh and helped himself to a mug and coffee. "What burned?"

"None of your business."

His son gave him a look, but not as sour as Ruby's. "What's up?"

Dave wasn't about to tell Justin he had a woman on his mind. "Breakfast—up in smoke."

Justin dumped sugar from the table in his coffee and stirred it with a used spoon.

The act had never caught Dave's attention, but it did this morning. He grabbed a clean spoon from a drawer. "Here. Don't be a heathen."

Justin wiped his mouth on his sleeve. "You sure it's just overdone eggs that's kinked your rope?"

Dave stuffed paper plates in the trash and put the skillet in the sink. "We gonna drive those cattle down or sit here and talk all day?"

Justin took his cup and clean spoon to the sink and lifted the napkin on what remained of Georgia's cherry pie. "Where'd you get this? Or is that none of my business too?"

Dave caught the tease in his son's eye, but he wasn't gonna bite. "Come on. Dutch is probably here already with his truck."

Not only did he have a herd to split and relocate to winter pasture, he had to figure out what he was gonna put in that pie pan before he returned it to Georgia on Wednesday.

If she agreed to meet him.

Chapter Six

A burning sensation danced from Georgia's fingers and into her arms—a lifelong reaction to unexpected excitement. Sheesh. If coffee with the pastor was exciting, she was worse off than she thought.

Dave's phone call seemed rather sudden. It was only Monday. Should she accept his invitation? It wasn't exactly a date. He wasn't picking her up and driving her the entire two blocks to Main Street. But if she met him at Stan's Creekside Café, everyone in town would know about it. Literally everyone. With a population of eight hundred souls, news spread like strawberry jam on warm bread.

She pushed away from her desk and went out to water her flowers.

"Good morning." The female half of her fellow tenants came down the other set of back steps and out onto the grass. "What a beautiful day."

Startled, Georgia squeezed the handle of the spray nozzle too hard, and water dotted the young woman's black pencil skirt and heels.

"Oh!" She jumped aside, hiking her black bag.

"I'm so sorry!" Georgia dropped the nozzle into the mums. "I hope I didn't ruin your bag. You look like you're headed to work."

"Nothing that won't dry. It's just a little water. And besides, today's my last day."

Wonderful. She offered her hand. "I'm Georgia Andrews."

"Kayla Ryan. My husband, Rick, and I moved in about two months ago."

Georgia was dying to know if Kayla had been fired or if she'd quit. And it was absolutely not one bit of Georgia's business. However, location was not off-limits. "Did you work in Pueblo or Colorado Springs?"

Kayla brushed droplets from her skirt. "The Springs. One of the reasons I'm not too upset about things. It's a tedious drive every morning and afternoon with all that road construction on I-25."

"Yes, it is. I'm glad I don't drive often to Denver or Colorado Springs. I work from home."

Kayla gave her an appraising look. "Do you enjoy that? Rick and I want to start our own business. He's an architect and I enjoy interior design."

Georgia immediately felt self-conscious about her half of the house, but Kayla didn't look around as if mentally redecorating. "Yes, I do enjoy working from home, but it's nothing new. I've done it for years, writing books."

As was often the case when people heard this, Kayla's eyes lit with wonder. "That's amazing—an author. What do you write?"

"Romance, historical and some contemporary."

The wonder slipped. "That's nice."

Kayla was soon on her way, the flowers watered, and Dave's voicemail still unanswered.

"Lord, help me know what to do. Should I accept his invitation? As a friend, of course, but what about the tongue-waggers?"

And why should she care a stitch about something she hadn't cared about before? Let the wagging begin.

~

Dave felt the vibration in his shirt pocket, but he had three heifers running up a ramp with a dozen more to go. His phone would have to wait.

By noon, he, Justin, and Dutch Raye had half the herd loaded and ready to haul to the lower pasture. God bless Raye and his hauling company. Driving cattle along a public road wasn't Dave's favorite thing, and it was just plain easier to truck them to Justin's for the winter.

His son reined in next to the loading ramp. "Raye's wife is cooking lunch for us. You wanna stop by?"

"Not today, but tell 'em I said thanks. See ya later." At the barn, he glanced at his phone, unsaddled Buddy, and turned him out.

She'd probably said no.

He stomped through the back door. Wouldn't she have called if her answer was yes?

Stalling, he fixed himself a fried-egg sandwich, then sat down at the table with the pie pan, the last of the coffee, and a deep sigh. "Thank you, Lord, for my son, this land, and this food." He looked out the kitchen windows. "The cattle and the church. Everything You've given me is good, Lord, because it's from Your hand."

He bit into his sandwich and opened the text message.

> Good afternoon. Thank you for
> the invitation.
> I'd be happy to have coffee with you
> Wednesday morning.
> I'll meet you at the Creekside
> Café at 8:30.

Relief made him almost weak. He read it three times before he could swallow. She'd agreed to come. He'd been so sure she'd decline that he was stunned. Like getting fifty cents a pound more for his cattle than the going rate.

That was it. That's what he'd put in the pie pan when he returned it—frozen beef.

He finished his sandwich and what was left of the pie, then opened the dishwasher.

"Whoo!" It'd been a while since he'd forgotten what was in there wasn't clean. He'd run it all through twice. Had to have that pie plate clean and shiny. It was awful pretty, like cobalt.

The next morning he chose four nice steaks, laid them in the pan, and wrapped it all tight with plastic wrap so nothing fell out. A close shave and starched shirt, and he was out the door by eight.

Ten minutes early, Dave parked a half block from the café so he could see when Georgia arrived. He looked at the plate of meat beside him on the seat, wishing he had one of those shopping bags with him. Was he just gonna waltz into the Creekside Café with a stack of raw meat?

Leaning over the back of the seat, he fished around in the half-cab for something he could carry them in besides an old feed sack. Doggone it, he wasn't as prepared as he thought. He got out and looked under the front seat and found a dirty rag and some old leather gloves.

"Good morning."

The pleasant greeting shot his head into the steering column and he almost swore.

"Oh, I'm sorry. I didn't mean to startle you."

He'd bet every last steak and the rest of the cow that a snicker edged that voice.

He rubbed his head, grabbed the pie plate, and covered it with his hat before turning around.

How could anyone with that sweet of a smile be so ornery? "Good morning, Georgia. You're looking well." Not the best greeting, but he wasn't clear-headed and didn't want to come on too strong.

"As are you, Dave." She covered her mouth, but her eyes danced with hilarity.

Dave checked for her Jeep but didn't see it. "Did you have to park out a ways?"

"No, I walked." She glanced at his hat.

"Walked? From home? I could have picked you up."

"Oh no. I'm only two blocks from here. I walk most mornings, just in the other direction."

He couldn't give her the pie plate now. He nodded toward the café. "Let's get some coffee."

He felt stupid carrying his hat rather than wearing it, but he managed to open the door for her and suggest a booth at the back.

She looked fresh and relaxed in cropped jeans and tennis shoes, more casual than Sunday mornings, and he thanked God again that she'd said yes. He waited for her to scoot in and then slid onto the seat across from her, setting the plate and his hat next to him. What was he going to talk about? Suddenly he was sixteen and didn't have a blasted thing to say.

Chapter Seven

If she'd known Dave Weatherford better, Georgia would have asked what he was digging for under the front seat of his pickup at eight o'clock in the morning on Main Street. And why he'd carried her pie plate with his hat on it instead of on his head.

Fortitude. She needed fortitude.

He ordered two coffees, then looked her in the eye. Dark and warm, his gaze searched her face as if looking *for* her rather than at her. "Would you like something to eat? A sweet roll or something?"

Fortitude fled. "That depends on what you have in the pie pan under your hat. Did you bake?"

He blushed.

Oh Lord, she'd embarrassed him, her *pastor*! "I'm sorry, that was rude. No, I'm not hungry, but please order if you'd like something."

He ran a hand down his face. "I didn't make a pie, but I didn't bring the plate back empty either."

The café's owner, Stan, redeemed the awkward moment and took Dave's order for two coffees and a cinnamon roll.

Oh dear. Georgia's stomach jumped up and down, waving its arms. How could she sit through polite conversation watching him eat one of those legendary, frisbee-sized delectables?

The answer arrived with temptation: two forks and an extra plate.

"Thank you, Stan." Dave answered his wink with a nod.

Georgia had been set up. Her hands tightened as she watched Dave cut the frosting-smothered roll in half, but they relaxed with a change of perspective. Maybe she should feel honored. He'd considered her stomach. Her shoulders loosened.

"Now I happen to know for a fact that it's impossible to refuse one of these cinnamon rolls, so like my granddad would say, just smile and say thank you." Dave pushed the second plate toward her.

How different he was away from the pulpit. Normal—whatever that was. Not pastoral, but not brash either. Polite. Thoughtful.

"Thank you. But now I'll have to walk twice around town and come into my place on the opposite side just to work off these calories."

He held his hand out to her.

Her breath stuck. What was he doing?

His eyebrows lifted in a question.

She gave him her hand.

And he bowed his head with a half-smile pulling at his mouth. "Thank you, Lord, for this great cinnamon roll and good company. Amen."

"Amen." A whisper, but there just the same.

"Dig in."

Georgia had always considered herself a confident, capable woman. She'd been on her own for five years and had faced every challenge with the Lord's unfailing help and strength. She'd even bought a house on her own. But here, sitting in a crowded café with a man she'd been thinking of entirely too much lately made her uncomfortable. As if God had been reading her mail and decided to go public with it.

"Have you attended Red Creek Springs Community Church for long?"

She cut a corner off her cinnamon half, unable to wait a second longer and buying time before she answered. What did it matter—

Heavenly! Oh my, this was better than she remembered. Her eyes closed in a sugar haze.

"That good, huh?"

She covered her mouth, full of the chewy, gooey goodness, and tried not to look like a pig. Or a prig. Maybe she should just relax and enjoy the treat. "About a year."

"So you're new to Red Creek Springs."

He didn't miss a bite but neither did he speak with his mouth full. She'd never dated a pastor before, so she wasn't quite sure of—

Wait. This was not a date.

"What brought you here?"

And there it was, the next turning point.

Georgia amended her earlier man-of-few-words judgment. "My husband died and I wanted to start over someplace new." She would never be able to recite those facts without her throat tightening, and she forced a sip of coffee past the lump so she could breathe.

"I'm sorry to hear that." Dave had set his fork down and looked at her with clear compassion, but not the gooey, cinnamon-roll kind. It was more of an I-know-how-you-feel kind. A straight shot from the hip, as she might say in one of her books.

"It's hard to lose a spouse." He picked up his fork. "Do you like it here?"

He might be an interim, rancher-turned-pastor part-timer, but he had good people skills.

"Yes, I do. I wanted away from the city and it's a nice, quiet town. A good place to write."

He tried his coffee and added another sugar packet. "I've been thinking about starting a men's breakfast group here one morning a week. What's your take on that? Do you think men would come?"

And he was asking her, a woman, because . . . ?

She took another figure-changing bite of cinnamon roll.

He watched her over his coffee. Her instincts said he had to be one of the most attractive, compassionate, and manly men she'd ever met. Well, maybe not the attractive part. She could see that clearly without any instincts at all.

"I do."

The one-sided smile. "You do?"

"I mean, you should try it." Her gut also warned that he was a witty tease, so be careful. "What do you have to lose?"

"Hmm."

Georgia considered that monosyllabic response from a man to be equivalent to a woman's "fine." She leaned in. "How many men have you invited?"

He matched her move. "Exactly zero."

The laugh escaped on its own, but a residue darted around inside her like a runaway puppy.

He feigned offense.

She deflected. "I take it I'm the only one you've mentioned it to?"

Another, longer sip of coffee.

"May I politely decline to comment further since I don't meet your qualifications? But you could ask some, oh, I don't know—men?"

He nearly spewed his coffee.

A couple of women from a table nearby turned to look at the commotion. Neither were from the church that she knew, and she smiled, acknowledging them with a nod. Much to her delight, they seemed a bit shocked. She barely contained a giggle. She hadn't felt this alive in a long, long time.

~

Georgia's easygoing delight set Dave on his heels. She was not at all the quiet and stoic woman from the next-to-the-last row each Sunday morning, beautiful to look at but hard to approach.

He lifted his hat from the pie plate and set the dish on the table. "I'm not a pie maker, but I do know something about raising grass-fed beef."

Shock and awe came to mind, but that wasn't his goal. However, the surprise on her face relieved all his misgivings.

"Oh my." She poked the two steaks on top. "And still frozen. Thank you." A glance, and her voice softened. "Thank you very much. This is quite thoughtful."

"Do you grill?"

A shadow slid through her eyes. "No. That was Jeff's specialty, and I don't like to go to the trouble for myself. Too much bother. And . . ." She turned the plate around.

"And?"

"The bird nest."

Had he missed something? "Excuse me?"

She glanced up as if confessing a horrible sin. "There's a bird nest in my barbecue grill. I haven't the heart to tear it out."

He coughed and cleared his throat, desperate to hide a hoot. His turn to be shocked and awed.

Her chin rose, but the light in her eyes contradicted her pretense. "It is not funny, I assure you. I'll not leave fledglings homeless just so I can have grilled beef."

"I see." He was losing the battle with the riot in his head.

"No, I am afraid you do not."

He shoved his hat on and scooted from the booth. "Well then, I'll drive you home and you can show me."

She hesitated and frowned at the plate of thawing steaks before conceding. "Oh, all right."

He left a large bill on the table—his quest to rectify Christians' reputation as stingy tippers—and opened the door for Georgia and then the passenger door to his pickup, taking the pan until she climbed in and fastened her seatbelt. "Here, you can hold this."

She was right about being two blocks from town. Exactly. He parked in front of a two-story, gray Victorian with a double front entrance, but couldn't make it around the truck before she had her door open and one leg heading for the curb. He reached for the pie plate.

Twelve inches shy of the ground, she grabbed his hand.

"Jump." That walking routine she talked about kept her in shape, and she easily cleared the gap. "If you want to put those in the freezer, I'll head around back and check out your grill. Is there a fence?"

"No, but follow me. The grill is behind the house under a small pergola."

He was beginning to think he might follow her anywhere, depending on whether she followed the Lord or merely talked the talk.

They passed an old, detached garage that had seen better days. The door glared like a sore eye, off one hinge and holding on to the other with the help of a cinder block. He started a mental fix-it list.

"There's the grill. There shouldn't be babies this late in the year, but there might be other critters hiding in there." She unlocked the back door with a key from her pocket. "One never knows."

Rolling his shirt sleeves, he looked around for a hat rack and settled on an empty flower-pot hook. Unintimidated when it came to "critters," Dave lifted the lid of the barbecue grill and there it was—one of the largest, most meticulously made nests he'd had the pleasure of removing from beneath overhangs and tractor hoods. He'd need a wheel barrow to cart off the litter.

Georgia came out wearing garden gloves and carrying a white garbage bag. "Thought you might be able to use this."

"Thank you. It'll hold some of it, but we may want to put most of it in a wheelbarrow and move it away from your deck here."

"Be right back."

He watched her walk to the garage and drag the cinder block out of the way. The door followed, swinging shut as she disappeared inside. She returned with an ancient wheelbarrow, complete with a flat tire. His list was growing.

Georgia wasn't one to sit and watch, and she pitched right in on the clean-up duty, more at ease than she was at breakfast, it seemed to him. Before the job was completed, he had an invitation to a steak dinner on Friday with one condition.

"You grill."

Chapter Eight

Georgia had gotten ahead of herself with the invitation for Friday, which was tomorrow. This whole affair was quickly getting out of hand. Tomorrow would be the third time in less than a week she and Pastor Dave had seen each other outside of church. Maybe if she kept reminding herself that he was her pastor, her flyaway imagination would settle down.

She put in another load of laundry and attached a wet cleaning cloth to her floor sweeper. But how could she *not* invite him back to grill a couple of those luscious steaks? They were certainly the last thing she expected him to return in her pie pan.

He'd spent an hour deconstructing the bird nest from her grill yesterday and cleaning up the litter. Then he cleaned the grill itself, and it seemed only polite to reward his labor with a good meal.

Baked potatoes, a green salad, and iced tea balanced the menu, with pumpkin bread for dessert since it was October. And what should she wear to a fall backyard barbecue?

Capris, of course, unless it rained. Or snowed.

The washer started banging itself across the laundry room floor, and she hurried to adjust the load. "This is exactly how I feel about seeing Dave." She pulled out a sheet and distributed it more evenly around the tub. "Out of balance."

After cleaning the downstairs floors, she transferred her bed sheets to the laundry basket and the wet towels to the dryer. Sheets always smelled better when they dried outside. Old-fashioned, yes, but some things could not be improved upon, and while she still had the crisp Colorado air-and-sunshine combination of fall, she would put that antique clothesline in the backyard to good use.

Adjusting the basket against her hip, she let herself out the door the same time as Kayla Ryan.

"Good morning." Georgia gave a brief wave, then headed for the line that extended from one side of her garage to a T'd pipe twenty feet away.

"Hi. I'm guessing that was your washing machine I heard earlier, bumping itself across the floor."

Georgia turned to see her neighbor a few yards away, dressed casually in cutoffs and a yellow midriff top. There had been a time . . .

"Yes, the old out-of-balance runaway stunt."

"Mine does that sometimes too, but now that I'm at home all day, I don't have to worry about it happening when I'm not around."

"That's right—how was your last day of work?" Georgia set the laundry basket down. "Unless you'd rather not talk about it. It's really none of my business." She lifted a corner of one sheet and clipped it to the line with a wooden clothespin.

Kayla joined her and did the same with the opposite corner. "I used to help my grandmother pin her laundry to an old clothesline—" She looked at Georgia with regret. "I'm sorry—I didn't mean to infer—"

"Oh, please, don't worry about a thing. It's nice to know I'm not the only one in town who knows what a clothesline is for."

Relief edged Kayla's laughter, and she helped Georgia pin the bottom corners to the second line a few inches from the first, creating a hammock effect with the sheet. They pinned the second sheet the same way.

"Thanks for your help."

"Clotheslines are also good for dogs. If you hook their lead to the wire, they can run back and forth as it slides."

"Great idea." Georgia picked up the basket. "Maybe I could tether my budgie out here for a bit of sunshine." She considered the twenty-foot line. "Then again, hawks and owls might think him a worthy tidbit."

"You have a budgie? A parakeet? I thought we couldn't have pets here."

"If you're renting, that's true. But I own this half of the house—like you would a condominium." She climbed the steps, leaving Kayla on the grass with her hands in her back pocket looking like a blue-and-yellow bird of paradise herself. "Would you like to see him?"

The young woman's face lit with a smile as she trotted up the steps.

~

A sense of purpose drove Dave through chores that morning. Not that he didn't always have a sense of purpose—he had a ranch to run and a church to keep going. But this was different. Longtime loneliness had slunk into a corner, replaced by a good woman's discerning spirit and willingness to help with a task. Her presence, even in his memory, gave him a sense of well-being and worthiness.

"It is not good for man to be alone."

Ruby rolled her eyes as if questioning his quotation of Scripture.

"Okay. It is not good that *the* man should be alone. What are you, a King James hound?"

The dog closed her eyes and moved her head to rest on the opposing paw.

He turned Buddy and a couple of other horses out to pasture, cleaned their stalls, and checked on a bay mare that had turned up pregnant. His granddad hadn't allowed mares on the place. But

Dave had found her at the sale and thought she'd make a nice little cow pony. He had no stallions, so he figured it was a safe gamble. Good conformation, gentle temperament. Kind eye.

"I could say the same thing about Georgia Andrews, but I doubt she'd take it as a compliment."

There'd been no mention on the sale papers that the mare was carrying a foal, so he tried to look at it from a positive point of view: two for the price of one. The vet wasn't certain, but he figured she'd drop sometime around Christmas, give or take a week.

Dave riffled through his workshop until he found an old tire pump and a rubber-patch kit, then loaded them and his tool box in the pickup. Tomorrow was Friday and he intended to take care of Georgia's wheelbarrow and garage door while he was there.

His heart kicked into a different kind of rhythm at the thought of doing something for someone else. But this was completely different than helping his son or a neighbor, or even filling in at the church.

It was personal. And he liked that.

Later at his desk, he wrote a list of names to call for the men's breakfast.

You should try asking some, oh, I don't know— men? A chuckle cut through the room's somber atmosphere. Georgia wasn't afraid to hit the matter straight on, and he liked that too. She didn't dance around him as if he were something special, but she didn't sidle up next to him either like some women had.

Five names made up his list. The top three were Fred Polk, Oscar Jeffers, and Daniel Bristow. Dave's gut cinched on that last name because he'd bet the north pasture that the guy had his sights on Georgia. Dave didn't know if he could maintain a preacherly demeanor with the coyote trying to run under him.

"Forgive me, Lord."

A couple of younger ranchers his son's age balanced out the list. It helped to mix the group, keep things from getting lopsided. How else were young men supposed to learn how to let the Lord into their everyday lives if the veterans didn't show them?

If all went as planned, this core group of men would invite others. Not that Dave wanted a crowd in the café's back room. A smaller group often felt safer and allowed for deeper sharing and the development of trust. But if two or three more came at the invitation of, say, the younger men, it'd make a great foundation.

But first he had to get Stan's approval. He grabbed his hat and truck keys and headed for town. He needed to stop by the feed and hardware store for a solar-powered gate opener and a small LP tank for the barbecue grill.

By Friday morning, he'd heard from all four men. Oscar Jeffers flat-out refused. Six a.m. was too early for him. Fred Polk agreed, and Daniel Bristow sounded downright happy about the whole thing. The two younger men accepted, which surprised Dave most. That gave him a nucleus of four, not counting himself. Not bad.

He shouldn't be so shocked by the miraculous.

Now all he had to do was keep himself occupied and distracted until five without forgetting to leave by a quarter till.

Chapter Nine

From the look of things in Georgia's back-yard, she was anticipating the barbecue as much as Dave was. An iron table on the grass with an umbrella canopy invited any and all to a picnic. She'd put a lot into it, with a checkered cloth, glasses, and a pitcher of something that looked like pink lemonade. He leaned over and sniffed. Strawberry.

Her back door opened and out she came with a foil-covered platter that she set on the grill's shelf. "You're right on time."

Her welcome made him glad he'd thought ahead and finished chores early. "Yes, ma'am."

"Help yourself to the lemonade and I'll be right back."

He followed her up the steps but at a safe distance, noting the handrail. Now *there* was a solution to a pending problem. "Can I carry anything out?"

At the door she turned and held it back. "Sure. I'd appreciate your help."

Her kitchen matched her Victorian house, aside from modern appliances. An antique oak table anchored the room and held stacked plates, napkins, and a bowl of green salad. He glanced around for pie but thought better of it and focused on a loaf of something near the stove and two foil-wrapped lumps he guessed to be potatoes.

He thought he smelled pumpkin. "You want these plates and the salad on the table?"

"Please. And if you don't mind, look in the door of the fridge and pick a dressing."

He laid a bottle of buttermilk dressing on top of the salad and carried everything out. The napkins matched the checkered cloth—a far cry from his catch-all dining table. Did she always eat like this—making everything look good? Or was this on account of him?

Clear reasoning deteriorated into wishful thinking.

When she went inside, he grabbed the propane tank from his truck, but not quick enough to beat her back.

"You are very observant. Thank you for that—we wouldn't have gotten very far without it, would we? I'm not sure when the tank disappeared, but it didn't matter since I wasn't using the grill."

"No problem. Just one of those details we sometimes overlook. Anything else to carry out?"

Hands on hips, she looked at the table, the grill, and back to the house as if she could see through the door. "I think this is everything."

He agreed. Everything he could want was right here in Georgia Andrews's yard. It had been a long time since he'd been so relaxed in a woman's company.

This late in the year, the remaining short hour of sunlight left just enough time to enjoy the meal and repair her wheelbarrow tire. No time to install the solar-powered gate opener for her garage door, but he did manage to replace the hinge screws so the door hung straight.

"My goodness, such a gift you have for repairs." She lit citronella candles scattered among flower pots beneath the pergola. "There are some things I simply live with rather than try to fix myself. I spend most of my outdoor time on my flowers and indoor time on my books."

He eased into a cushioned lounge chair, surprised that anything was still around to feed the bug zapper hanging from the pergola. In a couple of weeks, they'd all be gone.

He felt—at home. Not eating off a paper plate by himself and watching Ruby lick it clean. It wouldn't take much for him to stay right here all night, which he wouldn't do, of course. He cared more for Georgia's reputation than his own, and he'd do whatever it took to ensure it remained sterling.

She brought him a slice of pumpkin bread, joined him on a matching lounger, and put her feet up after kicking off her sandals. He had a sudden wild urge to hold those feet on his lap and rub them. Massage them after the day she must have spent getting ready for their dinner.

"Have you always lived in the valley?"

Her question snapped him out of his daydream, and he scooted back, dropping his feet to either side of the lounge chair. "I'm the fourth-generation owner of a centennial ranch. The original Weatherford homestead cabin is still out there, a little square-log house with a caved-in roof."

Her eyes lit with more interest than he expected, and he remembered someone had told him she wrote historical novels.

"Would you like to see it sometime?"

"Yes, I'd like that very much. Any local historical site is an important resource for my work."

Well, there was at least one more guaranteed non-date. "It's not far from the house, an hour or so ride."

She squeezed the arms of her lounger.

"Do you ride?" The distance might be too much for a novice.

"It's been a while, but yes, I do."

Relief pushed apprehension aside. "What about next Saturday?" He'd prefer tomorrow, but that might not be enough time. He already felt like he was on a fast course, and he didn't want to scare her off.

"I'll check my schedule," she said around a bite of pumpkin bread. "I don't mean to sound uppity, but if I don't stay current with my desk-top calendar, I'll overlap things that should not be overlapped. I'll text you."

"You don't keep your life in your phone?"

"No." An unapologetic sigh. "I'm old-school about some things and proud of it. Paper and pencil are often hard to beat."

"My son tells me I should write my sermon on a tablet. I tell him I do."

"Yours probably has lines on it, doesn't it?"

"You got that right."

Sharing a generational preference gave them something else in common, though neither of them was entirely off the grid. The conveniences of cell phones and computers were hard to beat. As she said, she'd text him.

Now he got to wait and see if she was just being kind, letting him down easy via her phone. Waiting was not his favorite thing to do.

He stood and slapped his neck for a critter that made it through the citron defense. "I better head to the ranch and let you get inside away from these borate bombers."

She stood, but no skeeters buzzed her. "Thank you for coming this evening—for repairing my wheelbarrow tire and rehanging my garage door." She fingered her hair behind one ear and then flipped it out again. "Oh, and for the steaks. They were quite a generous return for a mere pie."

"*Mere pie*?" he scoffed. "You don't want to taste what I can do to an innocent pie crust and a dish of fruit." There it was again, her liquid laughter. His insides warmed. "You do the pie, and I'll take care of the beef and wheelbarrows."

"Deal."

He hadn't shown her the gate opener, and he tucked that idea aside as an ace in the hole for another visit.

Georgia was especially pretty in the falling night and candle glow. Soft. Vulnerable, almost girlish in her summer top and cropped pants. Would she push him away if he gave her a parting hug? Would it be too forward? Would his congregants consider it inappropriate?

Doggone it, he and Georgia were God-fearing grown-ups. He'd not be ruled by fear of what someone else might think.

Before he could move on his instincts, she stepped closer, within arm's reach. Her voice quieted. "Thank you again for coming. I enjoyed the evening."

He reached for her and drew her in. No preacherly side-arm hug, but the real thing. "Thank *you*."

She fit against him as if made to do so, and her arms went around his waist, her head just beneath his chin.

Apparently, she meant what she said.

~

Georgia blessed the poor lighting. At least Dave couldn't see her blush after melting into him like she had. What was she thinking?

She was horrified, and it flared from her cheeks. How could she be so bold?

Of course, if this were a scene in one of her books, she'd not describe the lighting as poor. It was completely and unabashedly romantic.

And she was completely out of her mind. He'd said nothing that suggested interest beyond friendship, but she had crossed an invisible yet definitive line. *Because she had felt that tug in her heart.*

She picked up the salad bowl and dressing and went inside for a tray to carry everything else. Was this really happening to her—Georgia Andrews, widowed author of romance novels? Did people her age have romantic dinners in their backyard? Did other real-life, single women practically swoon when a man came over and actually fixed things that needed to be fixed? Without being asked.

Did they notice a crisp cotton shirt and jeans, or aftershave that made them want to nuzzle his neck?

From the kitchen, she walked slowly and deliberately to her desk, where she flipped on the light and checked her calendar. *Please, let next Saturday be empty.*

"Write, write, write."

"Not tonight, Jack. Go to sleep."

Next Saturday was blank.

"Thank you, Jesus."

"Jesus, Jesus, Jesus."

It was also the last day of October.

She ran both hands through her loose hair. Wasn't it August only the other day? How fast summer fled, with an hour less daylight now. Suddenly, it was fall. She just hadn't noticed it for the last thirty days.

The empty calendar space seemed to glow at her. It wasn't even anyone's birthday, at least not anyone she knew. No deadlines—yet. No appointments.

"Jack, I'm going horseback riding a week from tomorrow. What do you think of that?"

"Don't kiss that bird."

Reaching for her phone, she mentally framed a reply to Dave's invitation:

I'd love to go riding with you, and I can't wait until next Saturday.

"Georgia—pull yourself together. You're not a teenager."

"Pull together."

"Jack, go to sleep!" She grabbed the old towel on the back of her chair and covered his cage. "Lights out."

Flopping into her chair, she admitted she was drawn to Dave Weatherford. Unashamedly attracted to and interested in him. But she would not throw herself at him.

God would have to throw her.

She laid the phone down, grabbed the tray on her way through the kitchen, and gathered plates, glasses, and everything else from the table outside. Dave had already turned off the gas and closed the grill, and she picked up the long-handled steak fork and oven mitt. The last person to wear that mitt was Jeff five years ago, days before his stroke.

Her throat tightened. After all this time, tears still threatened at the oddest moments or over the silliest things. Visual triggers popped up when she least expected them, but memories were attached to everything. She'd lived a full life with the love of her youth, the father of her child. The man she'd made plans and woven dreams with.

A stroke was not in their plans.

A deep sigh quivered from inside her, and she hugged herself. She'd forgotten how wonderful it was to be held in the arms of a strong yet gentle man. To not be alone.

No, that wasn't it. She was never alone, but she was by herself—a very tangible and physical difference that she was growing weary of.

"Oh Lord, am I foolish to think I could love and be loved again? That I *should* love again. Am I being unfaithful to Jeff?"

Chapter Ten

Dave made it through the weekend and Sunday's sermon without any visible scarring, but the next five days nearly cost him his hair.

She'd texted him—thank God—to say yes, she'd ride to the cabin with him, so he spent the week cleaning his kitchen, den, horse stalls, and back porch—all the public places. The upstairs could wait, because nothing short of a heart attack would get him to let her up there.

Saturday morning, he readied Buddy and a gray gelding for Georgia. He took his best guess at the length of her legs and adjusted the stirrups, then left both horses at the hitch rail in front of the barn.

The bay mare was getting a belly on her, and he led her out to the pasture, where she rolled and shook her head, not sure, it seemed, about what was happening to her. A gentle thing she was, and young, but he hadn't ridden her much. He'd just had a hunch about her, that she needed to be on the place. That something good would come of her.

He prayed so.

The sound of an approaching vehicle turned his head toward a dust cloud crawling up the lane from the main road. Blades of early light cut through it from the east. He smiled.

Georgia Andrews wasn't afraid of sunup, and he guessed not much else either. She drove past the house and parked near the barn.

He went to open her car door.

"Good morning." A camera hung around her neck as she got out, ready for the day in boots, jeans, and a long-sleeved shirt. No hat, but she wore a genuine air of anticipation.

Inviting her had been the right call.

The last time he'd seen her, she had definitely hugged him back, and the memory spiked his heart rate. "Good morning. You look like you've done this before."

"Like I said, I've ridden. It's just been a while." She reached inside for a water bottle and a canvas tote, then closed the Jeep door. "Do you have saddle bags for one of the horses?"

"I can add some. What have you got there?"

"Just a little something to hold us over until we get back."

"Come up to the house and I'll get you a hat. I've got a few hanging on the porch wall. Something should fit."

She walked beside him, keeping up with his longer stride because he'd shortened it a bit. No sense making her jog.

Grateful he'd cleaned out the catch-all space, he watched her reaction to rows of boots, hats on hooks, and a set of long horns over the door to the kitchen.

She reached to touch it. "How beautiful. Was it one of yours?"

"No." He shook his head. "I just like the look of them."

"Me too."

So far, so good. "Pick a hat—any hat."

She tried on several and settled on an old straw hat that had seen better days. That stoic woman at the back of the church radiated life and the willingness to live it.

"Good choice. That was my son's favorite when he was a kid. Worse for wear, but definitely broke in. Come on and I'll introduce you to Sodaback."

She followed him outside. "That's an unusual name. Is it from a long line of bucking stock?"

"So, you know about bucking stock."

"I do write Western fiction. I've heard a little about it."

Her understatement sparked a dare in her eyes, and he guessed there wasn't a whole lot she didn't know about horses and the West.

"Sodaback's as gentle as they come. He's got an odd patch of white blotches on his back as if he'd been dusted with baking soda. The name stuck."

She approached the gray with her hand out, palm down. Bent close to his muzzle, she rubbed his neck, murmuring a few soft words. Not her first rodeo.

He brought saddle bags from the tack room and laid them behind Buddy's cantle, then tied on two rolled slickers just in case. Colorado's weather was anything but predictable.

Georgia left the gray long enough to stuff her sack and water bottle in one side of the bags and her camera in the other. After a long look at the eastern horizon, she returned to her horse and gathered the reins. "I love this time of day. Anticipatory, as if creation is holding its breath, listening for its Creator."

Her words sank into Dave's soul, quenching it as if he'd been waiting all his life to hear them. Could it be that the Lord was behind this whole thing?

"Then let's get to it." He loosed Buddy and swung up. He'd not insult Georgia by telling her what to do or offering her a leg up. Something told him she knew.

~

Some things were not easily forgotten, and horseback riding was one of them, learned when Georgia was a child.

"The stirrups are perfect. You have a good eye."

Dave nodded once and turned his horse away so she couldn't see his face. "Lucky guess."

She knew better. No luck about it. In fact, she didn't believe in luck and doubted that he did either. She'd heard enough of his sermons to detect the value he placed on God's direction. Not that God told him how long her legs were, but the Lord had definitely blessed him with the gift of observation.

She touched her heels to her horse's side and trotted up beside Dave's horse. They were heading straight for pine-draped hills that skirted a higher ridge. A ribbon of fading green ran along the edge. How she'd love to see those aspen once they turned.

Would the cabin be in the pines or lower on the grassland? Settlers and homesteaders built near a water source, but streams could have gone dry since then. The land often changed in a hundred and fifty years.

"I haven't been here in a while." Dave spoke casually, almost to himself. "Used to bring Justin here with his rifle and shoot tin cans off an old hitch rail. No animals around for him to accidentally cripple or kill."

"Justin? Is he your son?"

Dave looked at her then, his eyes still carrying a melancholy light. "Yes—yes, he is. Has his own place now, a couple sections south of here. We both run cows on this grass."

They'd slowed to an easy walk, and Dave's horse reached for a mouthful of tall grass. He checked it with a quick tug. "You know better than that, Buddy. Stop teaching Soda bad habits."

"It's beautiful here." Her voice felt almost intrusive. "So quiet I can hear the meadowlark's call as clear as a church bell."

He nodded, lost in his own private world for a moment before speaking. "Time stops up here. The craziness doesn't reach this place. It's cut off from people and towns and time schedules. Sometimes I wonder about my great-grandfolks and how they lived their lives—following only the dictates of their livestock and the seasons."

"No manmade deadlines."

He glanced her way with a huff. "I imagine you have your fill of those."

"Yes, but I've learned to outpace them by setting my own—about two weeks ahead of my editor. That way I have breathing room and I'm not as stressed when something comes up. And something always comes up, you know."

He made a throaty noise, not a chuckle but a warm sound she appreciated deeply. It resonated with assured strength in the face of uncertain times.

She knew ranchers weren't in it for the money—it had always been that way aside from cattle barons of bygone days. Other things drew them, like the love of the land, the cycle of give and take, living and breathing.

However, one didn't become a preacher for the money either.

These points said something about the man who rode next to her, tall and solid in the saddle, holding his reins with a light hand, and scanning the horizon beneath the brim of his hat like a hero from one of her books.

What did that make her? What role did she play in this story?

And then she saw it—before he pointed it out. Her hands tightened on her reins and her breath quickened. Maybe he wanted her to notice it, for he'd reined off to an angle so they approached the aspen grove from the east.

Only the shell remained with a roof caved in and ravaged by time, weather, and wildflowers. The cabin lay like a broken egg that once held life and now only memories.

Square logs framed a four-wall space, small by today's standard but with enough room for an iron bed frame, rusted cook stove, and a weathered table with broken chairs. She imagined a hutch could have once huddled against a wall, holding simple china and a bread bowl. Hooked rugs might have covered the dirt floor. The remains of a stone fireplace anchored one end of the cabin, and she sensed the reason Dave's home boasted the same.

Her horse blew and bobbed its head for a tuft of bunch grass.

"Are there snakes?"

"There are always snakes and, like guns, they're always loaded." Dave turned away from the cabin toward a clearing where he dismounted and dropped his reins.

Georgia followed, happy for a chance to grab her camera. "Do you mind if I take some pictures?"

"Nope. I thought you might want to, but I expected you to use your phone. I was surprised when you arrived with an actual camera."

"I use both, but when I want something reproduceable, I use my Nikon."

He took up position far enough away that he was out of her view most of the time, but she meandered around for different angles and managed to get a shot framing him through the cabin's open doorway. With him dressed similar to how his great-grandfather might have dressed, his thumbs hooked in his belt, it was easy to capture heritage in the picture, as though this cowboy had stepped through time to stand here today.

She wanted to know more about his past, his life as a rancher, and what led him to be a preacher too. "Ready for a break?" She walked to the horses and reached into the saddle bag. "Do you like banana bread?"

His face lit like most men's do at the query for food, and he overlapped two slickers on the grass. "It's not exactly a picnic blanket, but they'll do."

"They're perfect. It's not exactly a picnic."

From her canvas tote she retrieved the thermos and a foil-wrapped loaf of banana bread, still warm. She filled two tin cups and handed one to Dave.

"How did you become a preacher?"

He squatted on a slicker, and she couldn't prevent a smirk.

"What?"

"I'm sorry. You're so *cowboy*, that's all. Like someone out of one of my books."

"So your characters *hunker down*?"

At that she laughed outright and sat back with her legs crossed. "They do, just like that."

He settled and stretched his legs out. "My granddad knew God's Word so well it fell out of his mouth every time he opened it. He helped me see the Lord's touch on the land and wildlife. Offered to pay my tuition to Bible college. I went for a couple of years, but as he declined, my dad was left to run things alone. The ranch called and I couldn't let it falter in my generation. I came home."

Georgia gripped her cup with both hands, staring into its dark liquid, so like the color of his eyes. "And elders at the church knew your background."

He nodded and sipped his coffee.

Dave Weatherford was a rescuer.

"I sweetened it with honey," she said. "It cuts the acid."

He took a long swallow. "I like it."

Pleased by his approval, she unwrapped the bread and handed him a thick slice.

"This is still warm. Do you bake every morning?"

"No. Just when the Spirit moves me." She bit into a piece and focused her attention on their setting rather than the man in front of her.

"So now you're blaming God."

Their laughter and the pleasure in their voices skimmed the clearing and fluttered through the nearby aspen. How could she not fall for this cowboy preacher who fit her life so perfectly in ways she'd not anticipated?

Chapter Eleven

Georgia Andrews had a way of making Dave feel that he could be himself in her company. That she wasn't measuring his holiness or judging his sermon. Course, he wasn't preaching at the moment, unless actions really did speak louder than words. In that case, he'd have to agree with the old adage "Preach always—if necessary, use words."

Their surroundings certainly preached a sermon about God's fingerprint on every aspect of nature. Georgia seemed to pick up on it too, and she drank in their setting with a studied eye.

Like Val.

"My wife enjoyed it here before she became too sick to ride. We'd come up and bring a lunch, just enjoy the fresh air and sunshine."

Georgia didn't flinch at his mention of Val, and memories of her own brushed her face. "I can imagine that she loved it here. Jeff would have. Don't you think they're each enjoying an even more beautiful setting than this?"

The lump returned, and Dave couldn't say anything for a minute. He just nodded and looked around them, grateful to be spending time with someone who appreciated this place and also knew what it felt like to lose a spouse.

"If you don't mind my asking . . ." Georgia took a sip of coffee, giving him a chance to stop her. When he didn't, she asked quietly, "What happened?"

Not many people asked anymore because most knew. He gave the simplest answer. "Cancer. Two years ago."

She shook her head and averted her gaze, unwilling to barge in on a private matter. He appreciated her respect.

"Val hadn't wanted to go the chemo route. Her choice, and I honored it. Six months after she passed, the church asked me to fill in until they found someone permanent."

Georgia pulled her knees up and wrapped her arms around them, gazing into the aspen grove.

He took a chance. "You?"

She swallowed a couple of times, and he recognized the same lump effect. Should have kept his mouth shut, but he waited.

"It was a stroke. Almost five years now, but more sudden than your wife's suffering. One day Jeff was there and the next, he wasn't."

Something stretched between them in that moment, and Dave knew it could draw them closer if they let it. He wanted to let it.

She sighed. "Are you ever blindsided by a smell or a word or a sudden memory that pops up out of nowhere and twists you into a knot of tears?"

She'd nailed it so well he couldn't speak. Had to clear his throat a couple of times and take a deep breath. "Yeah."

She looked at him then with more understanding than he'd seen in others. She knew. They both knew. It was common ground beneath them, ground not traveled by everyone and littered with memories sometimes bright and sometimes as crumbling as the old homestead.

With two more slices of the best banana bread he could remember eating—no nuts—they finished the coffee and rolled the slickers.

"Any more sights to see while we're here?" Georgia gathered her reins and stepped up on Sodaback.

"I've got a view you might appreciate not too far from here. We'll ride along the edge of the aspen where a couple of low hills open to the valley. Maybe you'll see your house."

"Ha—I doubt that! How about the church? The steeple should stand out above all else except the water tower."

He led them east, skirting the aspen until they came to a flat spot. Reining in, he turned to face the valley and Red Creek Springs.

Georgia had kept her camera around her neck, and after drawing up close to him and Buddy, she took several pictures. "You're right. An amazing view." She worked the long lens, then handed the camera to him. "Put the strap around your neck, then aim at the town. You might see something you recognize."

He lifted his hat and looped the strap, knowing what he'd find. "There it is. Red Creek Springs Community Church. Red roof, steeple, and all."

"Click the shutter."

He took a couple of shots, adjusted the zoom lens, then turned and caught one of her. "Too close to get Soda in the picture, but it's a good one of you."

Surprised, she took the camera back. "Sneaky, I must say."

He reined away and headed for the ranch. "I've got someone at the ranch you might like to meet."

Georgia trotted up beside him. "Who, Ruby? I've already met her. Does she have a friend?"

"She's a bit taller than Ruby."

"A *she*. Okay. Could be a granddaughter or a filly. A puppy? Do you have a puppy?"

The woman made him want to laugh and shout all at the same time. He felt young—at least younger than he was. How could she do that to him simply by enjoying life?

~

Georgia hadn't expected the "she" to be a mare, and a mare in foal at that. This whole experience with Pastor Dave Weatherford was working out to be more unexpectedly invigorating than she imagined possible. Adventures like this happened to younger people. The kind who populated her romance novels. Yet here she was, drawn deeper and more strongly toward a man she had once feared was unapproachable.

The mare grazed in the center of a small pasture but came to the fence when they dismounted.

"Looking for a handout?" Dave rubbed beneath her forelock.

"What's her name?"

He shook his head and rolled his eyes.

"You didn't just roll your eyes." She bit the inside of her cheek.

"Yes, I did. Can't help it. Craziest name I've ever heard for a horse."

"So are you going to tell me or make me guess?"

"You'd never guess."

"I am a writer, you know. I name all the horses in my books."

He slid her a side glance, daring her to try.

"Come on, give me a hint."

"It's connected to Christmas and it's biblical."

She'd not expected that turn. This might be harder than she thought. "All right, how about Bethlehem?"

He scoffed. "No."

"Manger?"

"No."

"I'm sure it isn't Magi."

He threw her an odd look.

"Is it? Is it Magi? Wouldn't that be a better name for a gelding?"

"No, it's not Magi."

It wasn't Shepherd, Angel, Hosanna, or Gloria either.

"I give up. Tell me."

He faced her and leaned an elbow on the top rail. "What'll you give me in exchange?"

Georgia's heart suddenly lurched back to her high school years and she was sixteen again, about to be kissed by the coolest guy in her class. She choked.

Then she coughed and choked some more, until Dave was slapping her on the back and laughing so hard, he was coughing too.

With one hand on her chest, she raised the other. "Stop, please! I give up. I can't breathe!"

He took her by the elbow and led her to a long bench against the barn where he sat beside her. "I haven't had such a good laugh in too long, Georgia. You do something to me, woman."

That quick, the easy space between them hardened. Apprehension stiffened her shoulders. How she had enjoyed being with him today, just being herself with no pretense or nervousness. Now she didn't know how to act—she, a romance novelist!

This was no make-believe story with made-up characters. This was her life. Her very real life. No deleting a scene or rewriting a misspoken comment. Every word, every move, every gasp or tear counted.

He cleared his throat. "Sorry, what I meant was—"

"It's all right. I understand." She stood and tugged on her shirt so her hands wouldn't flutter as she talked. "I should be getting back. Thank you for a wonderful morning. I enjoyed it immensely."

He walked her to the car, opened her door as usual, then stepped back, his hat tipped up so she could see the shock and sorrow in his eyes.

And tomorrow was Sunday.

~

If Georgia didn't go to church, Dave would know why. If she *did* go to church, she'd have to find something else to look at during the sermon. And she'd have to sneak out the back door, avoid her friends, and make a run for the car. No matter what she did, she was sure to draw attention—either his or everyone else's.

This was why one did not spend extracurricular time with one's pastor.

"I can worship and pray here just as well as in that building."

She put her dishes in the sink and wiped off the counter.

What was she so afraid of?

She cinched her bathrobe tighter and tromped up the stairs to change.

On her way down, she ran into the answer to her question.

Her friendship with Dave was becoming more than a simple, shared comfort. It was swirling—yes, swirling—into a deep attraction, and that scared her on two conflicting levels:

What if she lost it?

And how could she be attracted to a man other than her husband of so many years?

~

"How can I be attracted to a man other than my husband of so many years?" Georgia's urgent whisper went farther than her friend's ear, and a woman three seats away in the pew ahead turned and eyed her. Oh, good grief, did she know?

"Let's meet for coffee tomorrow morning," Sue said. "Eight thirty at that new coffee-and-donut place and you can tell me all the juicy details."

"Shhhhh!"

This time, the eavesdropper elbowed her companion and they both looked.

But God's mercy shone on Georgia that morning, for visiting missionaries spoke, and Dave sat on the front row facing them rather than her. She put an extra twenty in the offering box by the door on her way out.

All day, he did not text or call her. She didn't know whether she should praise God or cry.

After a fruit salad and two slices of pumpkin bread for an early dinner, she went out to work in her flowers. The garage door swung open with ease, and she grabbed her garden basket of implements and a pair of work gloves. A mindless distraction, gardening. No need to think about anything other than whether a new green growth was a weed.

She knelt in the flower bed by the back steps.

"Hey there, Georgia. Beautiful day, wasn't it?"

Kayla Ryan slid her cell phone in her pocket and folded up a lawn chair.

Georgia hadn't noticed her sitting out on her lawn. "Yes, it was." She pulled on her gloves. "I enjoy these fall days much more than the heat of summer, in spite of losing daylight so early."

Kayla sat on her bottom step. "And you leave early every Sunday morning. Do you go to church?"

Guilt crawled up Georgia's throat. She hadn't once invited her neighbor to church since the young woman and her husband moved in. "Yes, I do. The Red Creek Springs Community Church. Would you like to come sometime?"

Kayla posed a thoughtful look and rubbed the back of her neck. "Maybe. It's just that you seem so content. I've wondered if it had to do with your faith."

Georgia sat back on her heels. "It does. Jesus has gotten me through some tough times."

"How can He do that when He's not really here?" The doubt etched into Kayla's face warned of a deeper, hidden concern.

"I know we don't see Him in the flesh like we see other people, but He's here. We don't see the heat either. Or the evening breeze, but we know when they're here. If we ask, God's Spirit is with us every minute of the day, in every situation. He's promised to never leave us alone."

Kayla swiped at a corner of her eye and looked away. "I'd like to believe that."

Georgia stuck her trowel in the dirt and considered the young woman. "Is there anything I can pray about with you?"

Kayla stood and brushed off her shorts. "Not—not right now." She climbed the steps and paused at her door. "But thank you. Maybe another time."

The door closed with a deceptively soft click. Nothing soft about what that girl was carrying, whether pain or worry. Maybe both.

Georgia put her hand rake and trowel in the basket and turned on the hose. Water showered from the sprinkling nozzle, washing the flowers, cooling them, and creating a fine mist that refreshed her as well.

She'd been so consumed with her own affairs that she didn't even notice that Kayla could be worried or hurting. "Please, Lord, touch her heart where she needs Your touch. Help me pay attention and be ready to talk about You when *she's* ready."

Georgia's cell phone rang from the kitchen, but only twice. By the time she ran through the door, it stopped.

Caller ID said Dave.

He didn't leave a voicemail.

Chapter Twelve

Georgia stalled, hoping she didn't cry as the coffee-art tulip on her vanilla breve stretched unrecognizably with her first sip. Salt in her latte would not be good without caramel.

Sue leaned in with a conspiratorial glimmer as she cradled a guiltless sixteen-ounce caramel macchiato in her gloved hands. November had come in like Frosty the Snowman.

"You know that everyone knows, don't you?"

"No, I don't know that." Georgia sipped at the tulip's stem. "And what do they know anyway? What are you talking about?"

She knew exactly what her best friend was talking about.

"You and the pastor."

Coming from Sue's rosy-cheeked face, it sounded like the title of a Christmas rom-com. Georgia took heart.

"How can they know? We've been discreet. And private." What could be more private than a horseback ride on Dave's centennial ranch ten miles from town?

"What could be *less* private than Stan's Creekside Café?" Sue pursed her lips and studied the foam topping her drink. "Stan's isn't very discreet either."

Georgia slumped, but not much. "Oh, I know. But remember when I told you I was going to cut myself some slack? Live a little."

"Yes, I do, and I think it's about time."

"But you just said—"

"That Stan's isn't private. I'm sure that's not news to you. But it's out there now. I just want you to be ready for the nay-sayers—which, by the way, are *not* me." Sue reached across the table and squeezed Georgia's hand. "He's a wonderful man—a believer, handsome, funny, not lazy. I'm so excited. Tell me everything."

"What are you, twelve?"

"No, I'm fifteen and so are you and you're crushing on Pastor Dave. Not that every other single woman in the church wouldn't do the same if given the opportunity."

An explanation like that could make Georgia's spring lilacs bloom in winter. But her friend knew what was at stake. She understood Georgia's theory on Eve's DNA and how it infiltrated Georgia's every molecule. Eve had never lived *without* Adam.

If God said it wasn't good for man to be alone, what must He think about a woman alone?

Of course, some women preferred it that way and they did quite well.

But some women were not Georgia and not Sue either, who lived happily with her husband of more years than they cared to talk about.

"He invited me to his ranch."

Sue's eyes nearly splashed into her macchiato. "No."

"Twice."

"When?"

"The Sunday after the Sunday I almost fell down the front steps at church. And this last Saturday." Georgia filled her in on the high points, which in Georgia's estimation were every single point there was.

"And he fixed the flat tire on my wheelbarrow and rehung my garage door so it swings open and stays that way."

"So he's been to your house too, *and* he's a handyman?" Sue held her cup with both hands and planted her elbows on the outdoor table where they huddled in heavy sweaters. "So why do you look like you just found a bull snake in your flowerbed?"

"Because in spite of wanting to share the remaining years of my life with someone, how can I be so interested in anyone other than my deceased husband? I feel like I'm breaking my vows or somehow being unfaithful to Jeff." Another sip. "And how can it happen so quickly?"

Their coffee had cooled enough that Sue took a long drink and then dabbed a thin, white mustache from her lip with a napkin. "My mama was one for clichés, but her best one was 'be careful what you wish for—God may surprise you.'"

"That last part is not cliché."

"It should be. Haven't you been praying for someone to share life with? Seems to me, prayer is a lot stronger than wishing."

Georgia sucked the entire tulip off her breve. "Yes, you're right. But the suddenness of the answer has me spinning. I want to make sure God is in this and it's not just my wishful praying."

Sue shook her head. "The Lord isn't going to lead you wrong. Just don't get ahead of Him."

"But what if I'm conjuring all this up and it's not real—just a fling?"

"The word *fling* insinuates certain activity—"

"Okay, poor choice of words. But at this age, I don't have time to be stupid."

Sue snorted and had to hold the napkin against her nose.

"Wanna hear the last thing he said to me?"

Sue bobbed her head.

"'You do something to me, woman.'"

Sue's eyes slid closed and years softened from her face as if remembering a sweet, young love from her past. With a sigh, she looked at Georgia. "Did that do something to *you*?"

"It scared the snot out of me and I ran."

"What?"

"Not literally. I walked like a grown-up, but inside I was running. Things had been going so well, but that one statement showed me the reality of what could be happening."

"So what does Ashton think about you seeing the pastor on days other than Sunday?"

Georgia glanced at a young couple walking past, arms looped tightly in the cold. "She doesn't know yet."

~

Dave was not a coward, but facing Georgia Andrews was as tough as looking down the barrel of a root canal, and a whole lot harder than telling his son about her.

"I have to apologize, that's all there is to it. And since she didn't answer my phone call Sunday evening, I have no other option but to go to her home and face her head-on."

Justin thumped him on the back and said, "I wondered what was going on with you the past few weeks. Go for it."

Dave stared at his son.

"Don't look so shocked, Dad. You don't need to be living out here all by yourself, and I'd be happy if you found someone. This Georgia sounds like a nice woman, from what you've told me this morning. Plus she can ride. That's one more hand to help us with spring branding and roundup." Justin hooted as he reset his hat and walked out the back door.

Dave had put off telling him but realized Justin's reaction set about half of him at ease. Now the other half better man-up and get on with business or just forget the whole thing.

Georgia's tote and thermos sat on the counter. She'd forgotten them last week when she made a run for her car. Dang if that remark he'd made hadn't spooked her. Spooked him too because he hadn't seen it coming. But it was true, doggone it.

He'd already washed the thermos and had no clue about what to put in the tote when he returned it to her. Then he remembered the gate opener.

He changed his jeans for a pair that didn't have dirt in the creases around his boots, then added a vest and a ball cap.

Ruby sat on her haunches and gave him the once-over.

"What do you think?" He turned around to face her.

She grunted and laid down.

So much for compliments.

As he drove out of the ranch entrance, he passed a bunch of wild sunflowers making their last stand of the season. They'd grown there every summer and fall since he was a kid, and they'd be gone in the next few days. He backed up, put the truck in park, and with his pocket knife cut a bouquet. The sunflower-stuffed thermos didn't look half bad.

The clock on his dash said two thirty. Perfect. He didn't want to arrive unannounced at mealtime, but since she hadn't answered his call yesterday, he figured he'd have more luck just showing up.

"Luck has nothing to do with it, Lord, I know that. Help me get my foot out of my mouth and maybe start over with Georgia. I'd hate to mess things up so badly that I lose her altogether. That is, unless this isn't Your plan for our lives."

He turned onto her street and his pulse double-ticked at the sight of her white Jeep in the driveway. She was probably working, but that couldn't be helped. He had to get this weight off his chest. If she rejected him, at least he could go on with his life as he had been. Alone.

He sure as heck wasn't going to start dating. If the Lord had someone for him, he'd just have to trust God to point her out.

He grabbed the tote and flower-filled thermos, then took the narrow path and approached the door on the left.

"Jesus, Jesus, Jesus."

The front sash window was opened about an inch, and there was no doubt he'd heard what he heard.

"Be quiet, Jack, I'm working here."

Jack?

Dave was tempted to peek through the window but didn't. The interim pastor didn't need to be reported as a peeping Tom. He rang the doorbell instead.

Footsteps approached from inside, and the door opened to a surprised and absolutely gorgeous woman wearing readers halfway down her nose and her hair in a knot held by a yellow pencil.

Like a middle-schooler, Dave shoved the thermos straight at her. "These are for you."

Georgia looked at the sunflowers, then at him. At the flowers, at him.

"Write, write, write."

She jerked her head around. "Shush, Jack. Not now."

Was she going to invite Dave in or slam the door in his face?

Fingering some stray hair behind her ear, she took the thermos and stepped aside. "Good afternoon, Pastor. Please come in."

Pastor. Dave's heart sank to his boots.

"You left your tote and thermos at the ranch last week, and I thought you might need them."

She sniffed the sunflowers, no doubt as aware as he that they didn't have a scent. "I love sunflowers. They are my absolute favorite."

At least she didn't hate them.

"They need water. I cut them on my way to town and didn't have a bottled water with me."

She turned and headed down the hall past an ornate stairway and into the kitchen. Uninvited, he followed.

She held the thermos under the faucet, then set it on the counter, arranging the flowers to her liking. Just like a woman. A characteristic he missed.

Lord, help him. He didn't want to push her away and he knew he was completely capable of doing exactly that.

"About Saturday, I—"

"Would you like some hot tea?"

"Peach tea!" came from the direction of the living room.

"Excuse me for a moment, please." Georgia took a cracker from a box on the counter and went through a side door to what must be a dining room.

Did she have a visitor? Someone else who was interested in her? It better not be Dan Bristow, though Bristow's voice wasn't that gravelly. Didn't sound like a child either. Dave went to the doorway, where he saw her draping a large towel over a bird cage.

Feeling like a fool, he managed to sit down at the kitchen table before she returned.

"Sorry about that. Jack sometimes gets carried away, especially if he thinks he has a new audience."

Dave let out a bucket of air. "For a minute there, I thought you had company."

She shot him a side glance. "Oh, he is. But sometimes he's a bit too much. That's why I keep the towel handy." She poured two mugs of hot water from a coffee maker, added tea bags, honey, and spoons, and set them on the table.

Dave smelled peaches as he raised the warm mug to his lips. *Sweet as Georgia.*

"As I was saying, about Saturday. I'd like to apologize for blurting out what I did and explain myself. If you don't mind, that is."

The stoic, regal woman from the next-to-the-last pew at church watched from across the table. "Did you say something you didn't mean?"

Oh, brother. He took his ball cap off and squeezed the bill into a tubular shape. "That's not what I mean—I mean—I meant everything I said, but it must have come out wrong, because you took off."

Dang, that wasn't what he wanted to say either—accusing her right off the bat.

She took a slow swallow, watching him over the rim of her cup.

Now or never, cowboy.

"Georgia, may I speak candidly?"

She dipped her head. "I thought you always did."

Just take me now, Lord, before I bungle the whole thing. When nothing happened, Dave took a deep breath. "I enjoy spending time with you, and I'd like to continue doing so. Aside from Sunday at church. How about you?"

Her eyes said little. Guarded, holding him at bay, unlike her demeanor at Stan's, in the meadow, and in her backyard. But the sigh that floated from her parted lips raised his hopes.

"I'd like that."

Forgiven.

She stretched her hand out, palm up.

He enclosed it in his. "Good." If he wasn't careful, he'd melt down right there on her kitchen floor.

"My sudden exit from our day at the ranch was not entirely your fault. Your words caught me off guard, that's all." She looked at their hands. "Things seem to be moving so quickly."

Her cheeks reddened and the blush endeared her to him. He squeezed her fingers. "I agree with you, they are. But I don't want to change that. I want to get to know you even more. Share the bits and pieces of my life with you and hear about yours."

Her shy smile nearly did him in. He wasn't this vulnerable when he was a seventeen-year-old high school junior with acne.

She slipped her hand from beneath his. "On one condition."

His throat tightened.

"That we pray when we get together. That we keep the Lord front and center. Because I really don't have time in my life for anything less."

If he kissed her right there at the kitchen table, she might change her mind and kick him out. He settled for retrieving her hand. "You got it."

Chapter Thirteen

"Mom, are you serious? Why don't you take a step back for a while. When you come for Thanksgiving, we can talk about it face-to-face."

Ashton was perfect for her job with the University of Kentucky. A clear thinker, capable of planning and executing anything that needed to be done, including orchestrating her widowed mother's life, which wasn't going to happen.

"This is your life we're talking about, Mom."

"Did you hear what you just said, honey? *My* life. I'm not putting it on hold until we talk about it in three weeks. I'm merely letting you know."

"Where did you meet him again?"

"We bumped into each other at church." Georgia covered a giggle because she wasn't going to share those details. Ashton would have the local sheriff running a background check on Dave.

"Did I mention he's the pastor?"

"Yes, but—"

"I'm not calling to ask your permission, sweetheart. I'm calling to let you know, keep you updated."

Silence.

"Why don't you come here instead? You could meet Dave."

"I can't get away this year, Mom, remember?" A long pause, and Ashton's voice shifted to a gentler tone. "I worry about you. It just seems so sudden."

"Don't worry about me, honey, pray for me. And five years isn't sudden. I want the Lord's will, you know that. But I hope you understand that in spite of my love for your dad, I'm lonely. And I don't think God's plan for my life is to spend the rest of it by myself."

Ashton's dogs started barking in the background, and the conversation ended with Georgia promising she wasn't on the fast track to disaster.

Dave's visit that morning had changed things. Intensified them, in a way. Their relationship was becoming, well, a relationship, and she wanted Ashton to know sooner rather than later. Something felt serious. Permanent. And Dave had added to it by keeping his promise to pray with her. Outside on the back steps, right before he took a cell-phone picture of her handrail.

He listened to her.

He remembered things she said and honored her wishes.

Was this a genuine side of Pastor Dave Weatherford or merely a make-a-good-impression side?

He also had a few surprises up his sleeve. "I'll return Thursday morning to fix your garage door."

"But you already did."

"There's more to it than the hinges."

She didn't walk around to his truck with him, but from the porch steps asked, "Do you have any old bananas?"

His stunned expression was priceless.

"If you do, bring them, and I'll make banana bread while you do whatever you're going to do to the garage door."

"You're on."

She'd watched from inside behind the sash window as he drove away, Jack at her elbow without the towel covering his cage.

"He makes me feel safe, Jack. As though I've known him for years, yet it's been only months. And we've been seeing each other for mere weeks. Could something this quick be the Lord's doing?"

"Lord, Lord, Lord."

"Exactly."

~

All four men showed up at Stan's on Wednesday morning for Dave's "Bible and Breakfast."

"Clever," Fred Polk said.

"Humph," groused Oscar Jeffers who must have changed his mind about getting up early.

"Works for me." Dan Bristow looked at Dave's neighbor's boy across the table. "What about you?"

Dillon Fletcher, a student at the junior college, paused briefly between scoops of biscuits and gravy. "Sounds good."

Did the boy's dad ever feed him?

"We'll start with the book of John. Read a chapter during the week, then discuss it the following Wednesday. I'll warn you though, it's a meaty book. We probably won't get through an entire chapter in one morning and that's okay. We're here to feed on God's Word, not race through the most important thing a person could read. However, we need to respect Stan's offer of this room by clearing out before eight."

"You take this seriously," Dillon said, wiping his mouth.

"I do. God's Word can be more than just the weathervane on your barn if you let it."

That afternoon, the building committee met in the church basement, and Dave showed them the picture of Georgia's handrails. Most agreed that a railing on the front steps was needed, and John Butler volunteered to head a subcommittee to purchase materials and work on the installation.

"Where did you take this picture, Pastor?" Mildred Cummings asked, as if it mattered.

Dave knew it would matter as soon as he answered. "Those are the back steps at Georgia Andrews's home here in town."

The look on Mildred's face could have fried bacon. Thank God He saw fit to send His Son and not a committee.

An hour later, the pastoral search committee let him know that he'd have the second and third Sundays of November off. Two candidates would be speaking those weekends, and the committee planned to "call" someone to fill the pulpit permanently after Thanksgiving.

Dave's preaching days at Red Creek Springs Community Church were numbered. He'd thought he would be happy about that.

On his way home, he stopped by the market and bought the darkest, ripest bananas they had, which matched his mood. He was gonna miss these folks. Not that he'd go to church somewhere else, but he'd miss talking to them as their pastor, opening God's word with them, encouraging them through hard times.

His appreciation of Moses and King David kicked up a notch. They'd both been shepherds before they were leaders. Not cattlemen, but similar when it came to watching out for those that couldn't always fend for themselves. Good training ground for watching over souls.

~

Georgia finished the first draft of her work-in-progress Wednesday morning, downloaded it to a flash drive, and took it to the junior college satellite campus to print a copy. It cost her a hefty donation to use their printer, but it beat driving to Pueblo and waiting in line at an office retail outlet.

That afternoon, she cleaned the kitchen, her dining room/office, and the garage, which she hadn't considered doing since moving in two years ago. "Cleaning" was a relative term when it came to organizing things in a building with a dirt floor. All of her plastic storage tubs sat on pallets, but it did help to tidy her garden bench where she kept her tools. The windows probably hadn't seen cloth and vinegar-water since installation in the late 1800s, so she gave them a go as well.

At least she felt better about her home, but she looked worse herself and spent the evening getting ready for Dave's arrival. Since the weather was cooling, chicken pot pie became the meal of choice—from scratch, of course. None of those frozen, chemical-laced pop-in-the-oven meals for her. Besides, her pie crust was unbeatable.

Thursday morning, she was up early to walk in the near dark, make herself presentable in jeans and a light sweater, and start a pot of coffee for Dave.

"Coffee, coffee, coffee," Jack called from the dining room. The crazy bird loved coffee and could smell it, Georgia was certain. He never said the word unless she brewed a pot.

"Hold your horses, Jack. I have to let your cup cool."

At a knock on her back door, Georgia feared Dave had decided to come early. She fluffed her hair and smoothed her sweater, then opened the door.

"Hi. I hope you're not busy."

Kayla Ryan's red eyes said everything, and Georgia opened her arms to the young woman, who sobbed against her shoulder.

"Come sit down. I just made a fresh pot of coffee." Georgia grabbed a tissue box from the counter and set it on the table, then took two mugs from the cupboard. Honey, cream, and napkins followed.

Kayla sat down and then blew her nose. "Thank you."

Why now, Lord? Georgia squirmed against her desire to have everything ready for Dave and her calling to comfort others with the Lord's words. Yes, comfort. It was her purpose, and she used words to fulfill it, whether written or not. "Do you want to talk about it?"

With a stuttered breath, Kayla looked around the kitchen as if someone else might be eavesdropping. "I—I'm pregnant."

Georgia's first inclination was to congratulate Kayla with a big hug, but those weren't tears of joy running down her face. "Is everything all right with the baby?"

Kayla's head bobbed, and Georgia breathed a prayer of thanks.

"But they're not all right with Rick."

~

Dave's sermon was ready for Sunday and it could be his last. Or his next to last.

After eighteen months straight with no time off, the realization of one or two remaining Sundays kicked a couple of bricks out from under him. Maybe he should put the men's group on hold. The new pastor might not be comfortable with him maintaining that type of leadership position.

Or he could keep going through November, break for December, and let the new guy pick things up in January.

He turned onto Maple and slowed to a stop in front of Georgia's home. Every other time he'd seen her, he had something to give her, and his empty hands felt big and awkward without something to hold. He'd forgotten the bananas.

Gripping the steering wheel, he looked at the gray Victorian home so elegant and tidy.

Would Georgia give it up to live on the ranch?

The question laid his heart bare to anyone who cared to look. "Guess I hadn't realized that's where I was headed, Lord, until right now. I want to marry Georgia Andrews. Take her home and make her my wife. Do life with her. Wake up next to her in the morning, have breakfast with her every day, and sit by the fire with her every winter."

And it'd been only a month since they started seeing each other.

As his hands squeezed the steering wheel, his eyes squeezed shut. "If it's Your will, Lord. Help me know. Don't let me rush into something I shouldn't. Please, let me know Your plan."

He'd left the gate opener in Georgia's garage, so he reset his hat, got out, and walked up the front steps.

It took a little longer for her to answer the doorbell.

"Good morning."

Her smile warmed him from the inside out, and he drew her into his arms as soon as he closed the door. They stood right there, holding each other as if one had saved the other from drowning. He wasn't sure who rescued whom. Maybe both of them had, each the other. All he knew for sure was that he didn't want to let go. Not ever.

"Perfect timing." Georgia's warm whisper circled his neck and spread through his chest.

"How so?"

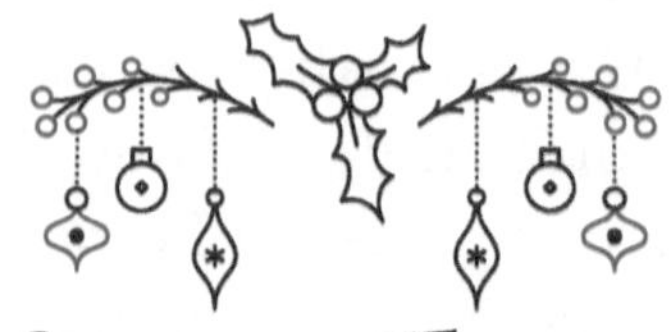

Chapter Fourteen

Georgia made another pot of coffee while Dave apologized for leaving the bananas behind. At least he'd remembered long enough to buy some. That counted.

"It's all right. I have some in the freezer in case of emergency."

"Is this an emergency? You mentioned perfect timing."

She pulled two rock-hard bananas from the freezer and clanked them into a bowl. "Not exactly, but your timing is perfect. You can pray with me about my neighbor, Kayla Ryan. She was just here, crying. She's pregnant and her husband isn't happy about it. He wants her to terminate the pregnancy."

Georgia glanced at Dave, and the same pain that had cut her heart sliced across his face. They were on the same page.

"I prayed with her and invited her to church again. I think she might come this Sunday."

Dave's brow creased as he took his hat off and hung it on the back of a chair.

"What is it?"

"This might be my last Sunday."

Georgia stared. "Why? What happened?"

"The search committee has called two candidates to preach the second and third Sundays of November. They hope to call a permanent pastor after Thanksgiving."

Her stomach clenched as if she'd been gut-shot—something that happened to the bad guys in her books. She knew Dave was their interim pastor, but she wasn't ready for another change. He was so good. How could the committee hire someone to replace him?

The coffee pot gurgled its dying drops into the pot and she filled two mugs. She needed something stronger than tea.

Rather than sit across from Dave, she pulled the chair around the table's curve and sat next to him.

He added honey to his coffee.

She added cream to hers and took the mug in both hands. "Do you want to stay?"

Maybe sitting close to him was a signal. Maybe it opened a door or lowered a barrier, for he reached around her shoulders, tugging her into him, his hand warm and strong on her right arm.

"It doesn't matter what I want." His deep voice came soft like she imagined the voices of her fictional heroes in their tenderest moments. "The church hired me to fill in until they found someone permanent. For several months, I've thought the sooner that happened, the better. But now I wonder."

She leaned into him, craving his warmth even though she wasn't cold.

He kissed the top of her head.

Oh Lord, help me keep my wits about me. With an answering pat of her hand on his chest, she withdrew a couple of inches to safer territory. "Would you pray with me for Kayla?"

Compassion and confidence merged in his consenting smile, and he took both her hands in his and bowed his head. "Lord, we lift Kayla and her baby to You. Keep them both safe. Shelter that precious child in the place you ordained it should grow. Be Kayla and her baby's defender and provider. Please speak to her husband's heart. Show him Your way and Your provision. Bring them all to You. In Your strong name, Jesus, amen."

"Jesus, Jesus, Jesus!"

Georgia's humiliation ran deep, but Dave's laughter displaced it.

"At least he knows who to call for help."

"Much to my chagrin." She gathered the mugs. "Want me to warm your coffee?"

Dave's chair scratched across the hardwood floor. "Save it for me. I'll finish it after I finish the garage door."

"What exactly are you going to do?"

He grabbed his hat. "Come on. I'll show you."

~

Dave's thoughtfulness astounded her. She'd not said one thing to him about her garage door—she'd not even complained about it in front of him. But here he was, rigging a solar-powered gate opener with a remote control. She'd be able to open and close her garage door from the comfort of her car. No more parking outside or wrestling with a heavy and resistive door.

He was amazing.

And he deserved the best banana bread she could make.

When he appeared to be almost finished, she left him with his tools and directions—which he had refused to consult—and went inside. She could get used to this, but if she was smart, she wouldn't. It was too soon.

Wasn't it?

The bananas had thawed nicely. She set the oven to preheat, then gathered ingredients as Dave came in the back door.

He washed and dried his hands at the sink, topped off his coffee, and leaned against the counter where she worked, one booted foot crossed over the other.

How could she concentrate in the face of such temptation?

She'd made banana bread countless times when Ashton was growing up. An inexpensive treat that filled her family with good things rather than preservatives. She'd always depended on the sweet smell to fortify memories of Mama-love.

A quick glance at Dave tipped his mouth on one side and set a warm light in his eyes. Much more of that, and she'd never get the bread made. She read the recipe three times to make sure she wasn't forgetting something.

Silently, Dave edged in, standing close enough to see in the bowl as she added flour, baking powder, and salt.

He watched as if she were creating the most delicious meal possible, and when she cracked an egg on the bowl, he asked where the trash was and deposited the shell.

She peeled one banana and then the other, dropping each peel into his open hand. After mashing them to mush, she stirred them into the batter.

"How do you know how many bananas it takes?" His rich voice kindled tiny sparks in her belly.

"I've made it a hundred times," she said, pointing to words penciled onto the stained page. "See that? Two bananas."

She slipped the pan in the oven and set the timer.

Dave turned her by the shoulders and drew her close, holding her gently, without urgency, without hurry. "You're a good listener."

She could stand like that forever, melding into him, warmed by his body and his breath on her hair.

Oh Lord, is this what I think it is?

~

"Show me where you work."

Dave's request came as unexpectedly to him as it did to Georgia, but she was gracious enough to grant it and led him into what had formerly been a dining room.

Jack eyed him from a cage in the corner.

With a mischievous look, Georgia introduced them. "Jack, this is Pastor Dave. Say hello."

The bird bobbed its head and side-stepped along its perch, then changed directions and bobbed in the opposite direction. It didn't say a word.

"Nice to meet you too, Jack." He held his finger to the wire-thin bars of the cage.

"I wouldn't do that if I were you. That budgie isn't a finger-sitter. He's a finger biter."

Jack cocked his head to the side.

Dave followed suit. "Thanks for the warning."

"I'll get you a cracker. He'll always take one of those."

Georgia returned with a saltine, a spoon, and Dave's coffee cup. "Slip the cracker through the bars, then hold a spoon of coffee against them. He might take a sip."

"He drinks coffee?"

"Loves it."

Danged if the bird didn't side-step over and reach through the bars with its beak. "I shouldn't be surprised. Ruby loves spaghetti."

"Ruby loves spaghetti," Jack mimicked.

Dave's laugh startled the bird and it flew across its cage. "Guess you have to be careful what you say around this fella."

"This is true."

Georgia had relaxed even more, and Dave suspected it had something to do with prayer. Ever since they'd started praying together, she'd been somehow different. A little closer, intangibly as well as physically.

"There's not much to see in here aside from my desk, computer, and books—of which I have way too many."

Shelves lined three walls of the room, all filled with books. "I imagine they're organized into sections so you can find what you want."

"Yours aren't?"

"Who says I have a lot of books?"

"You're a pastor." She turned for the kitchen. "I'll heat that coffee for you. It had to be cool for Jack."

The kitchen's fresh-baked aroma made Dave's mouth water like a snow-fed creek. "Come outside and I'll show you how to work your garage door."

"All right, but we have only fifteen minutes before the bread's done."

"Bring your keys if you want to park inside."

Georgia grabbed her keys off a hook and followed him out to the opener mounted on a post in front of the garage.

"Here's your remote, and here's a spare. It comes with two. Push this button to open or close. It swings out." He demonstrated.

She looked so pleased, he was actually proud of himself. "Not much to explain about a gate opener, is there?"

"Other than keep the snow from collecting on the solar panel." He glanced around quickly, looking for something else that needed repair. Any excuse to come back.

Did she have a lawnmower?

"Thank you for doing this. How about some banana bread, fresh out of the oven?"

"You're on."

"I'll bring it out. We can sit here and enjoy the sunshine. You never know when it will cloud over."

Dave relaxed in one of the chairs and scrutinized the garage. It could use a coat of paint, but it'd have to match the house. Time and weather had a way of changing the color.

Georgia returned carrying a tray loaded with plates, napkins, sliced bread, butter, and two cups of hot coffee.

He imagined her doing the same at his house. It wouldn't take much for her to transform it into a home.

Change was definitely in the air. Autumn was turning the trees here that had already turned in the mountains. Transition was coming to the church whether he liked it or not. And he sensed a change in his heart—a resurrected hope for someone to share life with, pray with, love.

"I already put honey in your coffee." She handed him the mug, pleasure in her smile as though she enjoyed serving him in that small way.

"You're a great hostess, Georgia." He bit into a slice of bread. "And a great cook."

Appreciation bloomed on her cheeks. "Thank you for fixing my garage door and wheelbarrow."

After he'd devoured a couple of slices with butter, Georgia wrapped the rest of it in foil and handed it to him. "Next time, the bananas are on you."

He took the warm package, determined not to wait until Sunday for next time. "Would you like to come out for a barbecue at the ranch?"

She hesitated so long, he feared she'd say no. "All right. What day and what can I bring?"

Bring yourself every day for the rest of our lives. "Tomorrow and make a salad. I'll come get you."

"What—and cheat me out of using my new solar-powered garage-door opener?"

Spontaneous laughter answered, but in the back of his mind, he planned to ask her tomorrow to come again on Saturday. Or maybe he'd just cut to the chase and ask her to marry him.

"About five?" Her innocent eyes had no clue what was going through his mind at lightning speed.

"Come earlier and I'll tell you the mare's name."

Chapter Fifteen

"Myrrh?"

"Myrrh."

"Oh dear." Georgia conceded it was an unusual name.

"Yeah."

She leaned against the mare's stall door with Dave. "I see what you mean about her name being associated with Christmas. Was she born at Christmas?"

Dave rubbed his jawline where a day-old scruff had sprouted. "I don't remember. Her birthdate didn't matter at the time. She just caught my eye as a nice little saddle horse."

"And the vet thinks she'll foal toward the end of next month?"

Dave nodded slowly, lost in thoughts she couldn't read.

"Your Christmas foal probably has a Christmas mama, with a name like Myrrh. What are you going to call the baby?"

He gave her the side-eye. "It sure as heck isn't going to be Frankincense."

She covered her mouth but couldn't hide a snort. "Oh, but Dave, if it's a colt you could call it Frank!"

His lack of humor on the subject only made it funnier.

The elevation of his ranch meant autumn arrived a week earlier than it did in Red Creek Springs. From his deck, where he grilled their early dinner, she saw the ribbon of gold that skirted the mountain. Her imagination flew to the homestead cabin and what winters there must have been like a hundred and fifty years ago.

Brought back to the moment by the delectable lure of barbecued beef, she turned to see him watching her with a hungry look. Disconcerting, but in a flattering way. She hadn't felt attractive in too long, and it was nice. Nice because she was confident of his honor.

He caught himself and turned the steaks, then looked off to the east. "Do you see that red line winding down from the hills and running across the grasslands? It disappears into that next dip."

She moved to stand next to him for a better view of the lowland. "Yes, I see it. Is that red color from scrub oak?"

"It is. You do your research."

"I have to if I want to get things right."

He laid his left hand against the base of her neck and squeezed slightly, gently massaging her shoulders. His warm strength was a comfort she'd forgotten. So was the electricity zinging down her back.

"So, Miss Get-It-Right, where do you suppose Red Creek Springs got its name?"

"Hmm, maybe from iron water coming out of a spring somewhere?" Her feigned ignorance gave her away.

"Nice try." He dropped his hand. "But I imagine you know the answer to that too."

"I'm guessing that red line follows a creek called Red Springs. The actual springs would be higher up, but it has such a nice ring to it, that people used it for the town's name."

"You win the first steak." He flipped one over, and coals sizzled beneath its dripping juices.

She'd brought her salad and dressing out to the picnic table on the deck, along with iced tea, butter for the baked potatoes, and a basket she'd found on top of the refrigerator that she filled with forks, steak knives, napkins, and paper plates.

"Grab a plate."

Three of the flimsy plates, if stacked together, worked well. She made two stacks.

"If I remember, you like your meat more on the done side of medium than rare."

"You remember correctly. I don't want my beef mooing." She held her plate-stack out and set the other nearby.

Eating at this time of day felt just right with darkness settling in so early now. The long, sunflower days of summer had been chased south by November winds. A similar wind had blown across her heart yesterday at Dave's mention that Sunday was his last day.

After his blessing, she cut into her perfectly grilled meat, wondering if they would continue to see each other or if he would pull back.

A cloud drifted across the late-afternoon sun, draining warmth and color from their surroundings, and she prayed it wasn't a harbinger of what was to come.

"What will you do the Sundays when the pulpit candidates speak? Will you be at church?"

He cut a bite and looked off toward the gold-rimmed forest before answering. "No, I won't be coming. I'm not involved in their appointment, and I don't want to influence people one way or the other. I'll take a couple of weeks off. Maybe drive up to Estes Park or down to Santa Fe."

The harbinger cloud settled in her stomach, turning the steak to stone.

"Will you spend Thanksgiving out of state?" Oh, how she'd love to invite him to her home and prepare a big meal like she used to, but she'd be at her daughter's in Kentucky.

She sensed him withdraw at her question, pulling inward like a turtle in its shell.

"I'll be home in time for Thanksgiving at Justin's—my son's. He's invited some of his friends over and threw a bone to dear old Dad." His features tightened. "You?"

She filled her mouth with buttered baked potato, giving herself a moment to check her emotions. Something had changed as swiftly as the temperature, and she wanted to cry. "I'm flying to Kentucky to spend it with my daughter, Ashton. She's hosting the family meal there for her in-laws and her husband's extended family."

The single cloud was soon joined by others churning over the mountains and the wind picked up, teasing paper plates and napkins off the table.

"We'd better get all this inside." Dave closed the grill and turned off the gas.

Georgia stacked as much as possible on the tray and carried it indoors. As she approached the kitchen, she glanced at the graceful longhorns crowning the doorway.

Would she ever see them again?

~

Georgia made her November 7 deadline with her publisher for the following year. Typically, she took a few days off before diving into her next book, but this time there was no diving. All she could manage was a belly flop.

She missed Dave so badly that she physically hurt. He had texted her a couple of times, but his words felt mechanical, at arm's reach. Had she lost him?

"Oh Lord, help me step back. Help me relegate Dave to the 'good friend' category and not grieve like this. I'm so weary of grieving."

Kayla had knocked on her door again and agreed to meet her at church the following Sunday. Georgia explained that the minister would be a visiting candidate. She wished that Kayla could have heard Dave's sermons, so applicable to one's life.

The candidate's message was well received, but Georgia missed Dave's personal touch with the people. Of course an outsider could not be expected to match that incomparable characteristic, and Georgia made a point of praying for God's will in the selection of a permanent pastor.

Yes, Dave was temporary. She knew that going in. But his replacement was one more change she resented. Another ripping away of someone dear. An unsettling of her routine.

Apparently, hers was not the only mind occupied with Dave Weatherford that morning. After the service, a clutch of gossipers stood off to the side, staring and whispering. One even tsked and shook her head, all the while eyeing Georgia. The only words she could make out clearly were, "She's after him, you know. Disgraceful."

Georgia prayed that Kayla hadn't picked up on it as they walked out together. Her writer-brain came up with a Jeep-load of witty comebacks, but she kept her mouth shut and repented for such thoughts when she got to her car.

This was harder than she thought it was going to be.

The next Sunday was just as bad, but she was glad to see that Kayla had returned and brought her husband. Oh Lord, hope reigned. Where was Dave when a solid male example was needed?

As Georgia left the church, one of the widow ladies approached. A quiet woman who served on various committees. "Georgia, do you have a moment? I'd like to share something with you."

Georgia expected a sermonette on the evils of seeing a man—the pastor, no less—instead of focusing on richer areas of her life. She expected the woman to say, "You're single for a reason." That might be true for many men and women, but too many times Georgia had heard it delivered like a jail sentence.

They stopped at the edge of the church yard, where frost-bitten mums had not yet been removed.

"I know you are living your own life and what you do is none of my business."

Amen.

"But I see the way you look at Pastor Dave—or did when he was here—and the way he looks at you. I also hear what one or two others in the church have said."

Georgia steeled herself for the attack.

The woman's expression softened and her eyes smiled. "God *is* love, you know. Why would He not give you love again?" With that simple question, she squeezed Georgia's arm and turned toward the parking lot.

Georgia had to consciously close her mouth.

The last Sunday of November brought Dave back to the pulpit and winter in on a razor's edge. Snow was rare this early in the season, but that had no effect on Colorado's weather patterns. In the Rocky Mountains, it snowed when it was good and ready.

~

Dave parked at the far end of the lot, behind the church. It was good to be back. He'd done a lot of praying over the last two weeks. He knew his withdrawal had hurt Georgia, but he'd needed to get away for a clear perspective, and he believed he'd found it.

He and Georgia fit. They complemented each other like warm banana bread and butter. Together they were better than each one alone.

The new handrails were well done, and he'd be sure to commend John Butler. After unlocking the front doors, he found the rock salt in the janitor's closet and scattered it on the steps and walkway.

A white Jeep pulled into the parking lot.

He watched until a woman with silver-streaked hair got out. She wore a deep-red parka with a fur-trimmed hood tossed back from her face.

The sight of her after so long nearly stole his breath.

Chapter Sixteen

When Georgia arrived for church in her snow boots and parka, someone had already salted the walkway and steps. Someone had also installed a handrail on both sides of the steps. Bless their soul and, more than likely, their aching back.

Anticipation churned within her as she labored to walk at a dignified pace. Dave had texted her, letting her know he was filling the pulpit on the last Sunday of the month, at the search committee's request. *I look forward to seeing you,* he'd written.

"Why didn't he call, Lord? I want to hear his voice." She chided herself for being ungrateful rather than thankful for small blessings. At least he hadn't forgotten her.

She sat in the second-to-the-last pew, and scooted over when Kayla and her husband came in a few minutes later. Such a bittersweet morning: Dave's last, and the beginning of Kayla's spiritual journey.

As was customary this time of year, Christmas carols were on the worship menu. Georgia loved them all—traditional hymns as well as the newer heart-tugging songs. The service ended with "What Child Is This" followed by an interruption from the search committee chairman prior to Dave's closing prayer.

"The last two weeks have been enlightening for us all, and the committee has canvassed the congregation regarding the hiring of a permanent pastor." Chester Stroble paused and looked at Dave before continuing. "We have voted unanimously to call a pastor who clearly has the Lord as his guide, one who values the Word of God and the individuals in the congregation. One who demonstrates genuine concern by acting on his convictions." Again, he turned to Dave. "You have served us faithfully and well," Chester continued, "even to the point of returning both Wednesdays during your break to meet with the members of your new men's Bible study."

Georgia was surprised but not surprised. It was like Dave to do such a thing even though it cost him time, money, and convenience to do so. What was wrong with these people? Why didn't they recognize what they had in him?

"Therefore, it is with humble hearts that we offer the permanent position to you, our own Pastor Dave Weatherford, if you will accept."

The sanctuary went silent. Dave clearly did not know this was coming.

Tears brimmed in Georgia's eyes at his shock, and she quickly wiped them from her lashes.

"However, there is one condition," Chester said, facing the congregation. "That Pastor Dave take ten days off twice a year, during the seasons of his choice."

People jumped irreverently to their feet, applauding as if they were in the bleachers at the high school football game. She joined them, Dave's personal cheerleader from the second-to-the-last row.

Finally, Dave joined Chester at the pulpit, where he accepted the call and wiped his own eyes. The pianist played a rousing rendition of "Joy to the World," and church was over for the day.

Georgia moved as slowly as she could, waiting until everyone had congratulated Dave, shaken his hand, and patted him on the back. She resigned herself to waiting outside at the bottom of the stairs until her stomach started begging for lunch.

The parking lot was almost empty when she turned at the closing of the church door.

Dave's smile melted her heart in spite of the cold, and she realized what was behind all her emotional see-sawing. She loved him. She truly loved him.

Bundled in a fleece-lined jacket and black cowboy hat, he joined her at the bottom step, the dearest man she knew. "I want to ask you something." His breath followed on a white puff.

She stared, conscious that her mouth was ajar. "What?"

"I want to ask you something." A tease curled his lip on one side and he took her hands in his.

Breath froze in her lungs and her pulse pounded. Could he hear it? Was her blood pressure spiking and turning her neck red?

"Will you help me pick out a Christmas tree?"

She nearly fainted.

~

Wednesday morning Dave awoke to six inches of snow on the ground and overcast skies. More snow was predicted for later in the day and the rest of the week. They might not get a white Christmas this year, but December would be blowing in on a snowplow.

Georgia had agreed to help him pick out a tree today, and he suspected she'd have plans for something delicious for them to eat afterward. Food was her love language, and he had no problem with that at all.

He'd also convinced her to let him pick her up and take her home later that day. Now, with the snowy roads, he was doubly glad. No doubt she could take care of herself, and the last five years were solid proof. But he was in the picture now, and he wanted to take care of her himself.

When he arrived at her house, the garage door was tightly closed and no tire marks led from beneath its old gray wood. But her back steps were swept and salted, and her door opened before he made it to the top.

"Good morning." Rosy cheeks and lips tempted him to kiss her breathless, but they hadn't quite reached that place yet and he didn't want to jump the gun.

"I'll get my coat and gloves if you'll take this basket out to your truck, please."

"Yes, ma'am." He went down the back steps. "Lord, help. I've got more temptation going on here than I've had in years. A day alone with a beautiful woman and a basket of homemade you-name-it. And if I were a gambling man, I'd say there's a thermos of hot cocoa in this basket too."

He set the basket on the passenger seat, then raised the adjustable console in the middle, leaving a place for Georgia to sit next to him. A fella could hope.

He locked the passenger door and closed it as she approached. "Come around and get in on this side," he said, obvious as a jay bird.

She complied. Gripping the wheel with one hand, she pulled herself to the seat and scooted over to the center. Her pretty lips bowed up with a secret behind them.

"Ready?" He started the engine, and warm air blew out from beneath the dashboard.

"Ready as ever." She shoved her hands in her pockets and hunched her shoulders.

"You cold?"

"No—cozy. It's nice in here."

The Boy Scouts' tree lot covered an entire corner parking lot on Main Street. Last night's snow dusted the trees, but the walkways were swept clear. Strings of lights crisscrossed overhead, and the whole place filled Dave with childlike anticipation. The last two Christmases had failed to win a second glance, and he had avoided trees and greenery like he would a bad case of measles.

"Oh, look!" Georgia seemed to glow with the Christmas spirit, and she hurried to a display of mistletoe strung overhead beneath a section of lights. Each white-berried bundle was tied with a red ribbon and clipped to the wire. "It's real mistletoe. I love it!"

Dave's imagination picked up speed and he steered the conversation elsewhere. "Are you getting a tree this year, or do you have a fake tree?"

Georgia's enthusiasm cooled and she shoved her hands in her pockets. "You mean an artificial tree?"

Whoa. Okay. "Yeah, an artificial tree." He still considered them fake and had been disappointed when Val had opted for one so she didn't have to vacuum needles off the carpet. A few weeks later they'd learned about her cancer. He couldn't help but connect the two.

"I used to insist on a *real* tree," she said. "One year, we even bought a living tree and planted it at the church we attended as part of their landscaping project."

"But . . ."

Her smile wilted. "My heart hasn't really been in Christmas the last few years, so I put up a small artificial tree in the front room by the window so its lights show outside." She looked at the bundles behind them. "But for some reason, I've always loved mistletoe."

"Isn't it toxic?" As a rancher, he was keenly aware of poisonous plants like wild iris and larkspur, prolific in Colorado. This kind of mistletoe didn't grow in the state, but they did have a dwarf variety, not as appealing as traditional mistletoe.

"It is if you eat enough of it." She stretched to touch one of the bundles. "But it's considered an evergreen, at least this kind. See how the leaves grow in symmetrical pairs? The romantic in me responds to that. Something about it speaks to renewal. And, of course, Christmas."

He counted twelve bundles before they wandered into the next row of trees, where they paused by a stately white fir. "My ceilings are ten feet, so I like a big tree in the great room. What do you think of this one?"

She had to tip her head back to see all of it. "Perfect. Do you have a star for the top?"

"I do. Will you help me get it up there?"

~

Georgia giggled. Giggled! What was wrong with her?

"I will if you let me stand on the ladder."

Dave put his arm around her shoulders and hugged her close. Another step had been taken today, and it lightened her heart. She refused to look too far down the road—nothing past Christmas. She prayed simply that this season would be a good one.

The top of the beautiful white fir stuck out past the tailgate on Dave's truck. He'd also bought a wreath for his door and one for hers. Surprisingly, he hadn't looked twice at the mistletoe, and it was a little disappointing.

No, she wasn't sixteen, but a woman's heart never outgrew romance. Especially at Christmas.

He backed up in front of his house, lowered the tailgate, and dragged the tree inside while she unloaded the basket she'd prepared. Hot chocolate, surprisingly still warm in its thermos; a package of small marshmallows; sliced banana, pumpkin, and orange-cranberry breads; and a plate of decorated Christmas cookies for the center of his kitchen table.

What a view the windows offered—snow-covered fields stretching all the way to bare aspen whose golden leaves had fallen so quickly this year. Such a Christmas-card setting with the blue sky, pine-forested mountains, and pristine snowfields. All it needed was a horse-drawn sleigh.

"Do you have time to stay and help me decorate the tree?"

His deep voice announced his approach from behind, and he wrapped his arms around her waist.

Romance-novel perfection right there, branding Georgia as the heroine. She squeezed his arms. "Absolutely. But not before I serve hot chocolate and cookies."

In keeping with Dave's penchant for paper table settings, she'd packed small plates with poinsettias and green napkins, but real Christmas mugs awaited the cocoa. God bless the dollar store.

"Do you have a tray we can put this on?"

He produced a thin, rectangular basket that worked perfectly, and they took the food and cocoa to the great room. He already had the tree in a stand with water. Several plastic tubs huddled at the edge of the room.

She handed him a mug of cocoa with floating marshmallows. "We have to start with lights first. Do you have lights for the tree?"

"I do. I also have red beads and silver beads, and more ornaments than I know what to do with."

Time, cookies, and slices of sweet bread passed quickly as they hung ornaments and talked about their respective Thanksgivings spent with their children. They talked of Christmases past with their spouses, sharing the good memories as well as the more painful. Georgia marveled that they could speak of their loved ones with ease and acceptance.

They shared a sense of comfort in their experiences and age. The insecurity of youth had sloughed off somewhere over the years, replaced by an acknowledgment of what was important now. The emotional ground between them grew firmer.

But what she wanted to know most of all was how Dave felt about the selection committee's request that he stay permanently at the church. So she asked.

He didn't answer right away, but carefully hung a small ceramic nativity on a branch, then stepped back for a wider perspective. "I have to admit I was surprised. I'd accepted my new position in a pew rather than behind the pulpit, though I was going to miss it. But it's God's business, after all. And it's His will that matters most, not what I think I want."

Georgia most definitely agreed with him and had come to that conclusion many times in her life, particularly since her husband had passed.

"It's a risky thing to say 'Your will be done.'" He spoke to the tree, but when he turned and looked at Georgia, she knew it was a double-edged message meant for her as well.

"Yes, it is," she answered softly. "It requires trust."

As happens too soon in winter's grasp, the sun slipped quietly behind the mountains.

"I need to get home. Jack will wonder what happened to me. But this has been a wonderful day. Thank you so much."

"Come out to the barn with me before we leave. I want to check on the mare." Dave tugged on his coat, hat, and gloves.

"You mean Myrrh?" She held in a chuckle as she zipped her parka and pulled the hood up.

He rolled his eyes.

"No, you didn't."

"Didn't what?" He stopped beyond the door, right under the longhorns, a perfect place for mistletoe.

"You didn't just roll your eyes."

He did it again and at her laughter, hugged her to him and led her outside.

Snow crunched beneath their boots, and when Dave slid the barn door open, the sweet perfume of hay swept around them. Low light spilled over a stall toward the back, and Dave slowed his steps as he approached.

"Hey there, Mama. How you doin' tonight?"

Georgia gasped at the mare's girth. "Do you think she's carrying twins?"

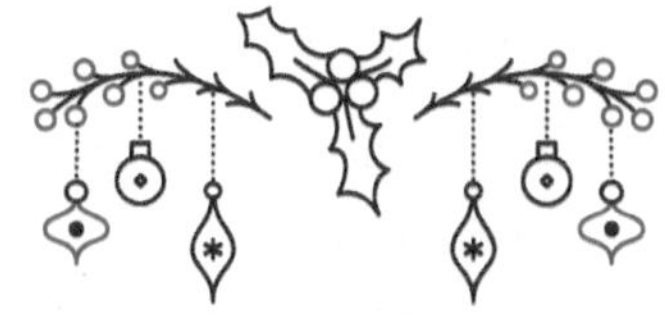

Chapter Seventeen

Christmas activities at the church took a lot of Dave's time, and Georgia didn't see him as often as she wanted. But baking and filling plates for neighbors along her street, wrapping and mailing gifts to Ashton and her husband, and starting her next novel filled her days.

Evenings were another matter.

She put on a sweater, turned the heater up a notch, and covered Jack's cage for the night. Her favorite slippers, hot peppermint tea, and a good book were her go-to comforts, and she settled into an overstuffed chair.

She had so much to be thankful for—a warm and peace-filled home. Her books and Bible. Yet the loneliness at night seeped in like rancid oil, tainting the blessings.

"Forgive me, Lord, for in my contentment with You, I still long for companionship with skin on. Someone to share life with. Am I wrong?"

Dave Weatherford had become a habit. A nice habit, but she wanted the Lord to direct this show, not her own longing or imagination. She wanted His will—as she and Dave had discussed.

For the past five years she had lived in the imaginary arms of her romantic heroes. Her work fulfilled her, kept her heart up, her head down, and her bills paid. But lately she'd grown restless, and once night fell she became even lonelier.

She knew she was not alone in the purest sense of the word. The Lord was with her, and she had sensed His presence even more than she had during her years of marriage. Solitude had a way of teaching her to listen. She'd learned the meaning of "Be still and know that I am God."

She didn't know the hearts of other widows, if they longed for companionship. But she'd heard some of them say they had no use for a husband or marriage. They were perfectly fine doing what they wanted, when they wanted, the way they wanted. A man would complicate that setup.

Georgia had tried to see life that way, but she was a romance novelist. Being single simply didn't work for her anymore.

And if things changed?

When Dave had asked her to help him pick out a tree, she expected him to propose. He hadn't even kissed her yet, so how could she think he was that serious about their relationship?

Yet she did.

"Can I give up my substitute comforts and routines, move from this house, and join my life with another?"

The answer whispered through her innermost being, soft as downy snowfall on a winter's day.

Yes.

~

Dave left the men's breakfast group and looked down one end of Main Street and up the other. No white Jeeps. He scrutinized every passerby and finally decided Georgia was not in town that morning. It might be his only opportunity. Slipping into the antique store, he glanced around. No customers. Perfect.

Next stop, the Boy Scouts' Christmas tree lot where he bought every bunch of mistletoe they had left. At least he didn't have to hunt for the real thing.

He didn't want fake—or *artificial,* as Georgia called it. No plastic or imitation décor. He wanted the real deal because that's how he felt about Georgia Andrews. She was the real deal.

He hoped the interest in her eyes and the warmth in her touch were more than friendly gestures. But he hadn't told her how he felt, and if he knew anything, he knew that was important.

During his two weeks off, he'd prayed as much about Georgia as he did the pastorate, and he felt confident in what he'd heard.

"Lord, help me get it right."

With Christmas Eve on Sunday, the day would be full with the regular morning service in addition to the evening candlelight service. Monday, he'd have Christmas dinner at Justin's, and he planned to invite Georgia.

At home, he built a fire and started hanging mistletoe everywhere possible: the front doorway, the light fixture over the kitchen table, the longhorns, the mare's stall, and a double bunch over the barn entrance. Every one of them was an opportunity to do what he'd been wanting to do for almost three months.

~

Christmas morning Georgia woke with childlike anticipation. The candlelight service had been tender and memorable, but she was eager for Christmas Day. She'd be having dinner at Dave's son's house. To her, it was the equivalent of being invited home to meet the parents.

Fresh pies lined her kitchen counter. Two cherry, Dave's favorite, followed by a pumpkin pie, and a pecan pie, which had been Jeff's favorite. The fruit of the field and the fruit of her hands. Her contributions to the big dinner.

She'd called Ashton to wish her a merry and blessed Christmas morning when an idea struck. "No, honey, I take that back."

"Seriously, Mom?"

"I *pray* you a merry and blessed Christmas. It's much stronger than simply wishing."

Next, she wrapped Dave's gift and slid it beneath a red towel in her picnic basket. The pies with their carrying covers stacked nicely on top. He would be by to get her at ten.

The front doorbell rang.

Looking down at her ratty sweatshirt and pants, she went to the door, trying not to be mad at him for arriving early.

"Merry Christmas!" Bundled and smiling brightly, Kayla handed her a bag stuffed with colorful tissue paper and pizzelles.

"What a surprise—thank you!" Georgia moved aside. "Would you like to come in?"

"No, but thank you. We're on our way to Rick's parents' with a special Christmas gift." She reached out and hugged Georgia tightly, then stepped back with misty eyes. "We're telling them they're going to be grandparents. Since we've been visiting your church, Rick has had a change of heart."

Georgia's eyes stung with new tears. "I'm so happy for you, Kayla. That's wonderful news. Praise God."

"Yes, exactly. Thanks to you, praise God."

Kayla hurried down the front steps and into a car, where Rick waited behind the wheel with the engine running.

Georgia closed the door and leaned against it, amazed once more by God's goodness and how He used the simplest things to deliver His message. She couldn't think of a better Christmas gift than what she'd just heard. And she loved pizzelles— one of the few things she didn't bake herself.

With enough time for a leisurely bath and extra attention to hair and makeup, she hurried into her office and removed the towel from Jack's cage. Leisurely was not on her menu that morning. "Merry Christmas, Jack. How would you like a piece of pizzelle for breakfast?"

"Breakfast!"

She broke a delicate, snowflake-like cookie in half, took a luscious bite, and poked the rest of it through the bars. It wasn't often that Jack had sugary treats, but at least these cookies had no frosting.

A quick shower, shampoo, and makeup routine left only warm clothing to choose, and she pulled on a pair of snow boots for good measure. Anticipation drove her like a race car, and she was ready to go and waiting by nine.

"Good grief, slow down. Christmas isn't going to disappear if Dave's late."

The doorbell rang at nine thirty, and she sputtered the water she was using to take her supplements. She lost all her lipstick wiping it from her face but managed to compose herself before opening the door.

He just stood there. Looking her over, from head to toe and back, his dark eyes full of longing.

Lord, help her.

"Merry Christmas, Georgia. You look fabulous this morning."

His voice was deep and soft, like a well-worn comforter, and she wanted to crawl inside it and curl up.

"Merry Christmas, Dave. Please, come in."

He stomped his boots on the mat but didn't remove his coat. Only his hat as he always did when he went indoors. "It smells good in here. Are you ready?"

Those two sentences didn't typically go together.

"Are you all right?" She touched his forehead and ran her hand down his cheek, and he caught it and pressed her fingers to his lips.

"Right as rain, as my grandad used to say."

He drew her into his arms and held her a long moment, warming her with more than his heavy coat. "I have something I want to show you before we go to Justin's. Are you ready to leave now?"

Reluctant to step out of his embrace, she inched back and looked at him carefully. "Yes, I can leave now. Is everything all right?"

"Everything is perfect. What can I carry?"

~

When Dave turned down the ranch road, Georgia's suspicions came alive. "Did the mare foal?"

The only answer she received was a big grin.

As they pulled up to the house, she noticed the wreath he'd bought on the door. It looked wonderful there, but something else quickly drew her eye. A large bundle of mistletoe that he had *not* purchased when they were selecting a tree.

Her own toes began to tingle. At the last minute, she opened the basket and withdrew the cherry pie that topped his Christmas gift, along with the gift.

"What's this?"

His obvious delight rewarded her efforts and reminded her that it really was more of a blessing to give than to receive. "One of these many pies is for you. Cherry."

That throaty rumble she'd heard before sent a shiver up her back.

"We'll leave it in the kitchen on our way through to the barn."

At his announcement, she expected to do just that, but he opened the front door only inches and stepped up on the threshold, where he stopped.

If she wasn't careful, she'd drop the pie and ruin everything.

But she didn't have time to worry, for he slid one hand under the plate, covering both of hers, and the other around her neck as he kissed her. Softly. Gently, but with a definite claim on her lips.

Oh my.

"I, um, the wreath looks, um, great. And, uh, the mistletoe. You bought mistletoe." She, the word-master, was stammering like a love-sick teenager.

Close to her ear, he whispered, "I'm glad you like it."

Grateful for his hand at her elbow, she made it over the threshold and into the kitchen, where Ruby looked up from her place by the table. Georgia hadn't thought to bring a pizzelle for the dog.

~

So far, so good.

Dave watched Georgia set the pie on the counter and pause there a minute. At least she hadn't kicked him in the shins.

If he wasn't mistaken, she'd fairly melted at the door. And he had several more stops along the way to the barn.

When she started around the island, he positioned himself at the table and drew her in as she approached. This time, she looked above them long enough that he captured her lips when she lowered her head.

Her arms went around him as a small sigh escaped.

With a hand at her waist, he directed her toward the back porch. As she stepped through the doorway, he tugged her red coat, and she immediately looked overhead.

Turning with a big smile, she threw her arms around his neck and definitely kissed him back.

It was even better at the barn door, but when they reached the mare's stall, Georgia grabbed him by the shirt and pulled him down—or herself up. He didn't know which and it didn't matter. He gave it everything he had and left her breathless.

Or it could have been her uncontrollable laughter that left her breathless, but he liked to think it was his prowess.

"See?" she said between gasps. "I told you I like mistletoe."

He turned her by the shoulders. "See?"

This gasp brought her hands to her mouth and a cry from her throat. "It's beautiful."

"She," Dave corrected. "She arrived last night and was waiting here when I got home from the candlelight service."

The mare nuzzled her long-legged daughter, whose tail flicked as she suckled, and a deep-chested whinny said all was right with the world.

"Mother and child at Christmas." Georgia's eyes assured him that he'd gotten it right. "What will you call her since you can't call her Frank?"

He laughed out loud and looped his arms around her. "Have any other ideas?"

"You could name her Mistletoe and call her Misty."

"Mistletoe and Myrrh. Has a *girly* ring to it."

"Sounds like the title of a Christmas novella."

"Okay, okay, come on. We don't want to be late for the big dinner, and I have one more stop."

"Stop?"

He took her hand and led her through the barn and into the house where fireplace logs had burned down to coals. "Have a seat and I'll stoke the fire."

Instead, she rushed to the kitchen and returned with a flat package wrapped for Christmas. "I have something for you."

Georgia Andrews was the prettiest, sweetest gal he could imagine in his home, and if things went like he hoped, she'd be staying on for a long, long time. He took a small box from beneath the tree and pushed his chair close to hers.

She held out her package. "You first."

Flat and rectangular, it could have been a book. But it wasn't, and he tore the paper away to reveal a framed picture of the old homestead, himself framed through the doorway, looking like he'd just walked out of the past.

"You're good," he said with a catch in his voice. "You've told a story in this picture. Thank you."

Pleased, her shoulders scrunched. "I was hoping you'd like it." She folded her hands in her lap and glanced at the little box he held.

It was now or never.

"You've changed my life, Georgia, and all for the better. Over these last three months, you've brought joy and laughter, and the fearlessness to live life with God's blessings, no matter what they look like." He held out the box. "I love you, and this is for you with all my heart."

The curly bow trembled as she carefully opened each side flap and slid the box out. Inside it was a second box, velvety green and rounded on top.

Her breath caught and she glanced at him with shining eyes. But when she lifted the hinged lid to reveal the contents, a small cry escaped.

Did she like it? Did she not?

"Oh, Dave, it's beautiful."

That's what she'd said about the horse.

"It's . . . it's mistletoe."

Scooting closer and holding it out as if he hadn't seen it, she touched each stone. "Look—the opal is a mistletoe berry, and the two jades on either side are the evergreen color of paired mistletoe leaves."

Lifting her eyes to his, she whispered, "I've never seen anything like this."

He took the ring from its nest and dropped to one knee before her. "It's like you told me—renewal. New life, starting over. Will you marry this ol' cowboy preacher, Georgia, and start over with me? Do life together and share what years we've got ahead?"

She offered her left hand, where he slipped the vintage ring on her finger in a perfect fit.

"Yes, Dave Weatherford. I love you too. I'd be blessed to be your wife and *do life* with you."

~

Georgia couldn't stop looking at her mistletoe ring, stunned by Dave's attention to detail and his ability to hear her heart.

A mile or so along the paved road, he turned onto another ranch road, graveled and leading south. It was a road she'd not traveled, and unwinding before them, it offered a new journey, a new adventure.

Sitting in the center of the bench seat next to Dave, she thanked the Heart-Watcher for bringing this man to her and taking care of her all these years. He knew what had lay ahead of her and had protected her from making the wrong moves along the way.

Continue to watch us, Lord, she prayed silently. Keep us in the path of Your choosing, for we love You and we trust in Your faithfulness.

~~~
~~~

A Boarding House Christmas

For by grace you have been saved through faith.
And this is not your own doing;
it is the gift of God.
Ephesians 2:8

Chapter One

Breanna Murphy squeezed her eyes tight against the invisible onion mist and prayed she wouldn't slice her fingertips off with the next few strokes. Why did she always get the job of dicing onions for her grandmother's sweet onion jam?

She rubbed her sweater sleeve across her watery eyes. Over the years she had tried everything to prevent the sting—from holding a slice of bread in her mouth to cutting the onions under water. Nothing helped, so she cried her way through the process. But this time, the onions served as a perfect cover for the waterworks coming from her heart.

Mollie padded into the kitchen and stopped at the stove to check on supper. She lifted the cast-iron lid from her stew pot, peeked inside at the simmering Swiss steak and then looked at Breanna. "You about finished with those rascals?"

"I'm on the last one now."

Mollie walked over and swept the onion skins and end pieces into her apron and peered into Breanna's face. "He's not worth those tears."

Breanna glanced at her surrogate grandmother and forced a shaky smile. "You're right. He really isn't. But it still hurts." How did Mollie always know if a tear was real?

"Well, there's plenty of fish in the sea—or deer on the mountain—as my Jim used to say." She emptied her apron into the wastebasket by the back door. "There are also several nice-looking young men at the church, I've noticed. You might meet someone there on Sunday."

Breanna's heart squeezed at the thought of Mollie's constant husband-hunt. She loved the woman dearly, the woman who had rescued her from Social Services and raised her as her own grandchild. Mollie and Jim were the only family with whom Breanna had ever felt she belonged.

"I never really cared for ol' what's-his-name anyway," Mollie said. She opened a lower cupboard door and pulled out another pot. "A little too wrapped up in himself, if you ask me."

Like a bad movie stuck on replay, Breanna's memory flashed the image of what Aaron had *really* been wrapped up in. She dropped the knife in the sink and washed her hands under hot water. "You don't know how right you are, Mollie. Better to find out now than later, I guess."

Mollie patted Breanna's back as she passed by on her way to the pantry. "Speaking of better"— the woman said from inside the small closet off the kitchen— "there will be one more for supper this evening."

Here we go already.

Mollie rummaged around, sliding cans out and in as if looking for some vital, hidden ingredient. "Remember that nice man down the road I told you about who helped me with my sink drain?"

Breanna knew exactly what Mollie was doing. This was the woman's standard way of broaching a touchy subject—casually, conversationally, from the security of the pantry shelves.

"He's a temporary boarder and has the room at the end of the hall upstairs."

No wonder Mollie was hiding.

"He bought the old Oxford place. Remember that beautiful barn? Fixing it up, he says." Mollie stepped out of the tight little room with a slight flush, as if she'd bent over and all the blood rushed to her mischievous face. "His furnace is out and he needed a place to stay until he can replace it. Naturally, I offered him an upstairs room."

Naturally.

"Besides, no one should be alone for Christmas, don't you agree?"

How could she not agree with this lovable, hopelessly romantic woman? As Victorian as the house she occupied, Mollie had always considered a well-planned romance a thing of beauty, and frequently said so.

"He's a cowboy architect. Complete with a horse and a drafting table he uses until he gets his computer set up, he said. And he's a wonderful handyman. He's helped me with quite a few repairs." She rifled through a large cutlery drawer for a manual can opener.

A cowboy architect?

"Let me do that." Breanna took the opener from capable but aging hands and set the metal tooth against the rim of the green-bean can. "I know what I'm getting you for Christmas."

Mollie looked up with the delighted grin of a child. "What, dear?"

"An electric can opener. This is ridiculous."

Mollie swept away the remark. "This old thing keeps my hands flexible. They have to be to turn it."

For all Mollie's pretense of living in the past, the can opener was about the only thing in her house that wasn't cutting edge. The antique wood-burning cook stove had been refitted with gas burners and oven, and the oak-paneled icebox door opened into a spacious refrigerator with a freezer below. Forced-air heat ran through every room, in spite of oak-mantled fireplaces upstairs and down, and a small sitting room on the main floor served as an office, complete with the latest desktop computer, printer, and cell-phone charging station.

Mollie pulled two strips of bacon from a refrigerated package and laid them neatly in a cast-iron skillet. As they sizzled, she added a little of Breanna's chopped onion and some freshly diced tomatoes.

"You could use a food processor, too. No more onion eyes."

Mollie ignored the suggestion. "Could you put some potatoes on to boil, please?"

Breanna gathered several potatoes from a bin in the pantry and rinsed them in the sink. She had to give her grandmother credit. The woman knew how to keep hands busy when a heart was aching.

~

Matt Dawson noted the white Jeep parked in the drive. He pulled in front of the yellow Victorian and left his pickup at the curb. Mollie's school-teaching granddaughter must have arrived. Home from Greeley for the holiday break with her fellow-teacher boyfriend. He'd heard all about Breanna and her other half—for whom his landlady had a keen distaste. He smiled to himself recalling how Mollie maneuvered every conversation around to her granddaughter. Her intentions were obvious, and he almost felt obligated to out-man the scholarly suitor spending two weeks at the Berthoud Boarding House. It shouldn't be hard—Matt had his degree in architectural design and his roots in ranching. But hopefully, his furnace would be replaced in a couple of days, and he could get back home for a less feminine Christmas.

Not that Christmas had ever been that important.

He wiped his boots on the front mat, opened the ornate door, and slammed into a wall of wonderful. His mouth watered. Maybe he could tolerate Mr. Education for a few days. Mollie's cooking surpassed anything he threw together, regardless of his campfire skills. He already carried an extra pound or two around his middle, and if he wasn't careful, he'd be letting his belt out a notch before New Year's Day.

"In the kitchen." Mollie's spry voice invited him down the hall, and he followed his nose to the homey room where two women busied themselves at the counter. Mollie faced him as she wiped her hands on her ever-present apron.

"Matthew Dawson, I'd like you to meet my granddaughter, Breanna Murphy."

The other woman turned with a peeler in one hand, a potato in the other, and a pained expression on her face. With one wrist, she pushed dark hair away from red-rimmed eyes and met him with a flat gaze.

"Hi. Nice to meet you."

The tone of her voice disagreed.

"Nice to meet you, too." For Mollie's sake, he'd play along. "I guess I should say welcome home. Your grandmother tells me you grew up in this house, and you come home every Christmas and summer."

Breanna turned back to the sink and tipped her head to one side. "Yeah. This is home."

Not very enthusiastic. Or welcoming. Drama queens he didn't need. He looked at Mollie who shook her head.

"Dinner will be ready in about half an hour, Matthew. That will give you plenty of time to clean up after your long day of whatever you do all day out at the Oxford place."

"Then I'll see you ladies in a little while." He backed toward the hall. "It sure smells good, Mollie. You're going to make a fat man of me yet."

The remark brought the desired lift to his hostess's mouth and a blush to her cheeks.

"Flattery will get you second helpings for sure, Mr. Dawson."

He took the stairs two at a time, thankful again that the boarding house had spare rooms this time of year. Motels were so cold and lonely. He looked through the open doorways as he passed the other two bedrooms. No suitcases or bags of any kind. No Mr. Teacher sprawled across one of the antique beds.

Didn't matter. Right now he needed a shower, a shave, and clean clothes. Sawdust had a way of working into his ears, nose, and under his collar, not to mention the straw-and-horsehair aftershave he'd picked up in the barn. At least he didn't have to share the upstairs bathroom with anyone. Yet.

~

Dining table conversation that evening centered on Mollie running into Matt at the hardware store.

"She was determined to unclog her kitchen drain herself," Matt said, "and insisted the clerk sell her—what did you call it?"

"One of those twisty things you stick down the sink to unplug it."

He laughed at the memory and waited for Breanna to respond, but her detached expression led him to believe she'd not heard the comment. "Even from two aisles away I could hear your resolve and felt obligated to rescue that poor clerk." He grinned at Mollie.

"Matt introduced himself as a part-time handyman, and said he'd be happy to check the kitchen drain." Mollie peeked at Breanna seated to her right. Disappointment weighed on the older woman's features, and her shoulders sagged as she patted her mouth with a napkin.

"She took me up on the offer, and I've been busy ever since." He recalled not only Mollie's generous offer of temporary housing, but also her bold once-over appraisal before agreeing to let him help.

After he'd unclogged the kitchen sink, Mollie had found various odd jobs that needed immediate attention, and she casually threaded her granddaughter's name into each repair request. His benefactor had also managed to milk every bit of personal history out of him. Almost. He'd withheld a couple of more troubling details.

He caught Breanna's sideways glance when the conversation lagged. He'd send no pity her way. She was being rude and self-centered. Mollie had done a lot to prepare for her arrival.

Then she reached for the mashed potatoes.

"These are so good, Mollie. Don't you want another helping?"

Maybe a little guilt had kicked in because the gal attempted a smile.

Her grandmother brightened. "Thank you, dear, I believe I will." She plopped a buttery serving on her plate. "You know, Matthew, Bree makes mashed potatoes as good as these." She passed the bowl across the table to him. "Maybe even better."

He helped himself and followed up with the customary brown gravy he hated to leave behind.

But the sooner he moved out, the better. He didn't need depressing female drama. He'd already lived through more than his share.

Chapter Two

Ten days until Christmas. Two hundred and forty hours. And another week after that before school resumed. Breanna had anticipated being home for Christmas, tucked away in a cozy, rural setting with magnificent mountain views and no school bells.

With Aaron and no dumbbells.

Now she doubted she'd survive the break from school—and the break from Aaron. Her heart needed major surgery.

She should have seen it coming. Instead, she had justified Aaron's excuses for spending more time at the gym on weekends and less time with her. He'd stopped bugging her to buy a membership, and she assumed he'd accepted the fact that she wasn't into working up a sweat pushing around resistive bars, levers, and weights. She preferred to walk or ride bikes, do something outdoors, not be cooped up in a room with a bunch of smelly people she didn't know.

When he missed their scheduled departure Friday evening, she'd swung by the gym to see if he was caught up in his weightlifting. He was caught up all right. In about a hundred and fifteen pounds of slick spandex-wrapped blonde hanging around his muscled neck. Breanna stood in the entrance to the weightlifting room long enough for him to catch her reflection in the mirrored wall.

It was worth the shock that rippled his face.

From the window seat in her room, she stared out at the snow-draped Rockies.

God's love is like the mighty mountains.

Mollie had told her that for as long as she could remember. The woman had made her feel wanted and loved right from the start. But rejection often lingered in the shadows, pointing a wicked finger, and whispering, "No one wants you."

She knew it wasn't true. Mollie and Jim had *chosen* her. They'd loved her and raised her to know that God loved her too.

But she'd thought Aaron loved her. And he'd chosen someone else.

In the bathroom, she dashed cold water on her face before going to the kitchen.

A china teacup full of coffee waited on the table, a handwritten list tucked beneath the saucer.

Mollie stirred something at the stove. "Good morning." She pushed a white strand into her upswept hair and smiled over her shoulder. "After you have your coffee and a good breakfast, I'll need your help with a few things."

Breanna slumped into a ladder-back chair, added cream and sweetener to the coffee, and picked up the list. She didn't know where the woman got all her energy.

"Breads, sweet and plain. Cookies, pressed and frosted. Deliver boxes for shelter." She sipped the coffee. "Take baked goods to church. Help paint upstairs bedroom—*what*?"

"What *what*?" Mollie said as she poured beaten eggs into a hot skillet of chopped bell peppers and onions.

"I'm supposed to help Mr. Fix-it paint? Come on, Mollie. This is my vacation."

"Did you have something else planned for the next two and a half weeks?"

Breanna looked at her diminutive, workhorse grandmother. A perky bow sprouted from her waist, testimony that Mollie starched even her apron strings. The woman had been born a hundred years too late.

"Well, do you?" Mollie peered over her shoulder.

"No."

"Good. I can use the help. It takes a lot of work to keep a place like this going. Especially during the Christmas season."

"Do you have other guests coming?"

Mollie scooped the cooked eggs onto a china plate, sprinkled grated cheese over the top, and set it on the table. "You never know, dear. Unexpected things have happened before."

Breanna scoffed. Guilt peppered her as she did the same to the eggs. Mollie was nothing, if not generous, and Breanna resolved to change her attitude.

"Are these chores listed in any particular order of importance?"

"They're not *chores*, but that's a good question. Let me see." Mollie poured herself a teacup of coffee and joined Breanna at the table. "We must bake before we can deliver, so that will be the first job. We don't want the house smelling like paint for Christmas, so that should be done early in the week." She scrutinized Breanna over her cup. "What do you think?"

Breanna wasn't about to tell her what she thought—that Mollie was deliberately pushing her at Matt. It irritated her, but she wouldn't hurt the woman's feelings. She'd simply have to suffer through the not-so-casual encounters. The same way she suffered through slicing onions.

"Of course you're right about the baking. I can start on that this morning." Breanna dug into the eggs. "Aren't you eating?"

"I ate with Matthew. He's an early riser and loves my Denver omelets." Mollie blinked sweetly from across the table.

The fastest way to Mollie's heart was through her cooking, that was for sure. "Denver omelet?" Breanna assumed a school-girl pout. "I didn't get ham in mine."

"And you're shoveling them in like a lumberjack." Mollie took her cup to the sink. "More coffee?"

"No thanks. If I'm going to get any spare time, I'd better start on that baking as soon as possible." She picked up her plate and at the counter, pulled her grandmother into a hug. "I love you, Mollie."

"I know you do." Her grandmother returned a tight squeeze. "I love you, too, and I want to see you happy."

Breanna took a step back. "I thought you wanted to see me busy."

Mollie laughed and tapped her finger on the end of Breanna's nose. "That's what I said. I want to see you happy."

That had always been her grandmother's philosophy and no doubt explained why she was so alert and healthy at her age. She kept on the move and always had some project going.

Breanna opened the apron drawer and pulled out a jumper style that slipped over her head and tied in the back. She might as well dress the part as long as she was here.

"Not that I'm interested, but for the sake of fairness, did you have a list for Mr. Fix-It too?"

"Oh, absolutely. I have so many things that require a man's touch, and he's perfect for all of them. I need to take advantage of his abilities while he's here."

How long would that be? Maybe he'd be gone by the end of next week, and Breanna could relax and be herself without feeling like a single-female display.

She found the big crockery bowl on the top pantry shelf and set it on the counter. Flour, sugar, canned pumpkin, spices, raisins, and other ingredients soon filled the extra space. She started with sweet yeast dough to let rise while she made pumpkin, banana, and zucchini bread. This afternoon she'd punch down the dough and braid it into a Christmas wreath before baking it. Then she'd top it with drizzled butter-cream frosting and red and green candied cherries.

"Deck the halls with boughs of holly," she sang softly as she kneaded the dough, plopped it into the bowl, and covered it with a thin tea towel. Even though she helped her third graders make paper chains and caramel-corn balls for their classroom tree each year, it never felt like Christmas until she started baking with Mollie.

Breanna looked up to find the woman wearing a secretive smile on her pink lips.

"What?"

"Nothing, dear. It's just good to hear you singing." She smoothed her hands down the front of her apron. "Think I'll go upstairs and pull out the decorations. I sent Matthew to get a permit so the two of you can cut a tree tomorrow after church."

Before Breanna could reply, her grandmother disappeared down the hall humming the familiar Christmas tune.

Chapter Three

How'd he get himself sucked in to this? That little gray-haired woman could charm the bark off a tree. And he was the proof, because here he was, standing in line at the Forest Service office for a tree-cutting permit.

"I don't want one from the nursery, and I don't want one from a tree lot," Mollie had said before he'd left this morning. "I want a *forest* tree, like my Jim used to get. They smell better."

Matt grumped at the memory and folded his arms across his chest. A little girl in line ahead of him scowled over her shoulder. "Daddy," she tugged on the hand she was holding. "Is that cowboy Mr. Scrooge?" The father threw an apologetic glance at Matt. "No, sweetheart. He's just been standing here for a long time. Like us."

Matt had never been called Scrooge before, but at the moment, the name fit. He'd driven all the way to Fort Collins to get the permit and now stood in line behind a child who called him names. This wasn't how he planned to spend his Saturday afternoon.

"Next."

He moved forward and listened as the father requested a permit for tomorrow.

"I'm sorry, sir, but if you want to cut a tree this weekend, you don't have to come in here. Just drive up to the site past the Red Feather Lakes area and—" She reached under the counter. "Take this brochure." The clerk produced a colorful trifold and pointed out the necessary information. "Follow this map. You can pay your ten dollars right there, but you have to be out of the area by four."

"Thank you."

"And, sir, you just made it under the wire. Tomorrow's the last day for cutting Christmas trees this year."

Matt stepped forward before she could say "Next."

"I'll take one of those brochures." Required reading before he headed out to cut the perfect tree for Mollie.

She slid it across the countertop, aiming a frown at his hat.

"Thanks." What was it with everybody today?

~

On the twenty-mile drive back to Berthoud, Matt plotted the next day's trip. He'd have to leave as early as possible to make it to Red Feather Lakes with enough time to find the right tree, cut it, and drag it out to his pickup. He'd scanned the brochure and noted the "Four-wheel-drive or chains" requirement.

Mollie had tried to give him gas money for this tree-cutting expedition, but he'd refused. Their agreement was room and board for labor. He snorted. She was definitely getting the better end of the deal.

When he got to Berthoud, he stopped by the appliance store to check on the furnace he'd ordered. It still wasn't in. Figured. Starving, he pulled into a fast-food drive-thru and ordered a burger and fries. Not exactly Mollie's cooking, but it would have to do. His mouth watered at the greasy aroma as he unwrapped the burger and bit into the juicy meat and cheese.

"Augh!" Mustard and pickles. He never ordered mustard and pickles. He'd specifically said mayo, lettuce, and cheese *only*. He shoved the rest of the burger into the bag and devoured the fries. By the time he parked in front of the boarding house he definitely felt like Scrooge.

As he opened the front door, a warm ripple of homemade bread and cookies roped him in. His mouth watered again, and Scrooge vaporized.

"In the kitchen." Mollie either had perfect hearing or radar.

Breanna stood at the counter. Apron strings joined in a knot across her lower back. Just above her great-fitting jeans.

"What smells so good?" He pulled out a chair, counting on Mollie to offer a cookie or two or three.

"Homemade goodies, of course." She headed his way with a platter of samplings and returned a moment later with a glass dish of whipped butter. "Honey-butter," she said, handing him a small knife. "You'll like it."

Afraid that he might be drooling, he wiped his mouth on his cuff. "Don't have to ask me twice. Thank you, ma'am." He slathered on the creamy stuff and sank his teeth into a warm slice of white bread. "Hmm."

"Good?" Mollie's eyes twinkled as she gave him a napkin.

"Great."

"Would you like some coffee to go with that?"

"Also great. How'd you know I was starving?"

"You're a man," she said. Men are always hungry."

Breanna turned around and rubbed her hands down her apron. Flour smudged her chin and one cheek, but her eyes sparkled. Clear and gray like the sky over the mountains at dawn. "So are third-graders."

Was that a smile lurking behind the flour? A big change from last night.

Matt repaid Breanna's near-smile with a look of near-offense. "I resemble that remark."

She giggled. "Now you *sound* like a third grader." She pushed up her bangs with her wrist and frowned at the platter in front of him, pointing. "Try that dark slice there and tell me what you think."

"Gladly." He could taste the pumpkin before it reached his mouth, and the brown sample melted away behind his lips. "Greath."

"What?"

He swallowed. "Sorry. Great. Can I have more?"

"May I have more."

"Sure, here." He held the plate out to her.

"No." She laughed. "I don't want it, you do. But it's 'may I' not 'can I.'"

He choked at her classroom reply. "Excuse me, Miss Murphy, ma'am. I thought school was out for Christmas."

She narrowed a gun-muzzle gaze. "Proper English is never on vacation, Mr. Dawson."

"Okay, you two, enough." Mollie whisked away the platter with one hand and made brushing motions at Matt with the other as if sweeping him out of the room. "That's all for now. You'll spoil your supper."

He drained his coffee and set the fragile cup and saucer in the sink. "Do you have any mugs,

Mollie? I'm afraid I'm going to break these tiny things every time I use them."

"This is a Victorian-era boarding house, Matthew. No mugs." She cast a warm smile in his direction. "Now out. We have work to do and so do you. I couldn't quite reach all the decorations in the east bedroom closet upstairs, and I need you to bring the boxes down for me. Can you put them in the dining room, please?"

He snatched another slice of pumpkin bread from the platter and shot a quick look at Breanna. Her mouth curved up on both sides.

"Anything for you, Mollie." He held one finger to his lips and raised his brows at Breanna in a plea for silence.

On his way up the stairs, he wiped his hands on his jeans and savored the last bite of warm pumpkin bread, wondering who made it.

~

Breanna swirled green frosting on a tree-shaped cookie and laid it with others on a strip of waxed paper. Dinner smelled wonderful.

"We'll eat in the kitchen tonight," Mollie said. "With all those boxes in the dining room, we can't pull the chairs out." She opened the oven door and with a thick mitt, slid out the top rack, and tested the pork roast with a fork. "Bre, would you please run up and tell Matthew that dinner is in half an hour?"

Breanna showered the tree cookie with sprinkles. "You need a megaphone or an intercom system."

"No, I need you to do me the favor." Mollie eased the oven door closed and laid the mitt on the counter. "Shoo! You can finish those and set the table for us when you come back down."

Breanna dusted off her hands, removed her apron, and draped it over a chair. Her heart raced as she mounted the narrow stairway, and she attributed it to her lack of exercise. Mollie really did need a megaphone. She eyed two wallpapered bedrooms on her way to the end of the hall. The woodwork looked okay to her, at least in passing. That painting request had to be another ploy at mixing more than colors.

The door at the end of the landing stood open, and the plush runner swallowed her footfall. She cleared her throat, announcing her presence.

"Yes?" A deep voice queried from beyond the door.

"It's Breanna. Sorry to bother you." She stopped at the threshold and took in the frilly room. Matt perched on a stool at a portable drafting table set in front of a west window. His large frame and rugged profile seemed out of place, like an answer to her students' favorite activity of "What doesn't fit in this picture?"

"Mollie wanted you to know we'll be eating in the kitchen. The dining room is too crowded with all the boxes."

He laid down his pencil and faced her, shirtsleeves rolled to his elbows, a shadow of beard hugging his chin.

"Thanks. Please—" He swept a hand across the room in welcome. "Come in."

She took one step in, stopped, and peered at the table. "A new project?" She slid her hands into the back pockets of her jeans. "Mollie said you're an architect."

"Freelance. Come see." He turned to the drawing and bent the snake-neck lamp closer to his work. "I don't have my computer and drafting programs here, so I'm going old-school until I get my place livable."

Feeling suddenly shy about being in his bedroom, she eased a little closer and stopped a foot or so behind him.

"These are my plans for the ranch house."

Blue lines and angles and perfectly square block print covered the large white sheet. In the lower left corner an artist's drawing revealed the finished product.

"That looks nothing like the old Oxford house."

"Good." An easy smile tucked a perfect parenthesis in his left cheek. "That's the idea." He smoothed a hand across the paper. "The bones are good, so most of the renovations will be cosmetic. Other than the furnace."

"You've had trouble getting one?"

"Getting what I want. It's taking longer over the holidays with so much bad weather in the east. I could probably find an import cheaper and quicker, but I want this place to be 'made in America,' as they say."

She regarded his dark eyes. "That's something I talk to my students about, at least as much as they can understand." He certainly was easy to look at.

"Did you make that pumpkin bread?"

The question startled her, and she felt her cheeks bloom in their typical self-conscious blush. "Yes. I do all of the Christmas baking. Our tradition, I suppose." She turned toward the door.

"You do it well." His rich voice fanned the flames on her cheeks.

"Thank you." She paused and laid a hand on the doorframe as she looked over her shoulder. "Dinner's in thirty minutes."

~

It was way too warm upstairs.

Breanna tugged at her sweater on her way down the steps and sent up a silent thank you for her downstairs bedroom. How could Matt even think about furnaces?

The distinctive aroma of sweet onion jam wafted out of the kitchen, and she involuntarily squinted.

Mollie stirred a batch on the stove. "Hand me that little pink serving bowl, dear." She turned off the burner and reached for a ladle.

Breanna held the bowl as her grandmother dipped. "Why do they call it jam instead of relish?"

"The way it's cooked, I imagine. And it's supposed to be served cold, but I've always preferred it warm." She set the dish on the cloth-covered table and added a serving spoon.

As Breanna laid out three china plates, she wondered about the bachelor status of her grandmother's latest boarder. An educated cowboy with a freelance job and a real home instead of a bunkhouse?

She sniffed. Of course he didn't live in a bunkhouse. Was that even done any more? But more importantly, why was a guy like him single? What history hid behind that stubble-chinned, dimpled face? Mollie no doubt knew the answers to these questions and more, but Breanna didn't dare ask. The matrimonially-minded woman might funnel Mendelssohn's *Wedding March* through her computer speakers during dinner.

At twenty-six and solo, Breanna already felt conspicuous. She didn't need to be singled out like the zebra in red goulashes that hung above the coat hooks in her classroom.

Knife, fork, spoon. She laid a sterling threesome at each place. Mollie believed in using the good china and tableware. "Why save it for guests?" she'd said. "Family is more important."

Family had always mattered to Mollie, yet she'd had so little of it. Jim died a few years after Breanna joined the Murphy household. Since then, she and Mollie had been each other's family.

And Matt? Why hadn't he gone home for Christmas?

His footfall on the stairs quickened her pulse as if she'd been caught thinking of things off limits. She looked up as he stopped in the doorway.

The dimple winked.

Afraid her questions streamed across her brow like a weather update on TV, she turned away.

"Sure smells good," he said.

Did he go to the gym like Aaron? Breanna doubted it. He struck her more as the outdoorsy type. Chopping wood, building fence. Riding, roping, and all that. Herding cattle. Even with the architectural degree.

"I do believe that's everything." Mollie headed for the table with a platter of pork roast and sweet potatoes.

Mr. Outdoorsman joined them and pulled out a ladder-back chair.

Breanna took the seat across from him, and Mollie sat at the head.

"Shall we pray?" Flushed from the heat and hurry of cooking, Mollie pushed a fluff of white behind her ear and held out a hand to either side. "Bree, would you do the honors?"

Breanna took her grandmother's hand and looked at Matt whose arm reached nearly the width of the small table. She rested her fingers in his and closed her eyes.

"Thank you, Father, for this wonderful meal and our guest. And thank you for Christmas here at home and what the season really means. Amen."

Her fingers warmed from his touch, and she feared her face registered the sensation.

"What is this," he said reaching for the pink Depression-ware bowl.

"That's my sweet onion jam." Mollie said. "It goes on the pork. Try it."

Breanna saw by the worry lines on his forehead that the name alone was enough to cause doubt.

"It tastes much better than it sounds." She raised her chin. "And I put a lot of work and tears into those onions, so you'd better at least try it."

Realization flickered. "So that's what you were doing yesterday afternoon. Slicing onions." He spooned out a polite-sized helping and passed the bowl to Mollie.

Among other things. A small sigh escaped her lips, and she sat up straighter, determined to keep Aaron out of her thoughts tonight. No doubt, she wasn't in his.

"Matthew, what did you find out about the tree today?"

He speared a slice of meat and handed the platter across to Breanna. "Tomorrow's the last day to cut, and I have to be up there, done, and out by four."

"Then we need to go to the early service. It's at eight thirty. That should give you plenty of time to make the trip." Mollie accepted the platter from Breanna and gave her a commanding look. "Be sure to dress warm. It's a little colder at Red Feather Lakes than it is here. But I'm sure you remember that."

Matt's loaded fork stopped halfway to his mouth and his eyes locked on Breanna.

He doesn't know I'm supposed to go.

Breanna coughed and reached for her water glass, feeling like that red-booted zebra. "You know, Mollie, I'm sure Matt can handle the tree cutting. We still have a lot of baking and frosting to do—"

"One more day won't hurt. It's the Lord's Day, and you should be out in His big, beautiful world enjoying it." Mollie reached for the copper-colored yams.

"I'll enjoy the company."

Breanna caught Matt's smug amusement and resented it. She was a grown-up. She made her own choices. Then she glanced at Mollie, and guilt wiggled up under her breastbone. What would it hurt to humor the woman?

Matt's comment sounded sincere, but his condescending smirk annoyed her. She'd seen that expression on little boys who thought they had everything figured out and didn't need her help with their math.

"Don't worry, I won't slow you down."

Laughing eyes betrayed his enjoyment at her expense, but a mouthful of roast and onion jam short-circuited his attention. His facial muscles relaxed, and he leveled his gaze at her. "This is really good."

Told you.

Matt reached for the pink bowl and helped himself to a second spoonful. "About tomorrow, Mollie."

She continued eating. "Yes?"

"I won't be making it to the eight-thirty service, but I'll be ready to leave when you and Breanna get home."

Breanna watched her grandmother from the corner of her eye and waited for the customary correction she issued when someone didn't do as she expected. The correction didn't materialize.

"That will be fine, Matthew. We won't be late."

Breanna coughed and nearly choked on her napkin trying to hide her surprise. She stared at Mollie. Did she not feel well? What happened to her usual sweet-as-sugar, stiff-necked reproach? She looked at Matt, who was shoveling in sweet potatoes and roast, oblivious to what Mollie's response should have been.

After a few moments of lighter conversation about the Christmas decorations, Breanna finished her dinner and helped Mollie clear the table, marveling at the dexterity with which her devious little grandmother chose her battles.

Chapter Four

Sunday morning Matt considered not shaving again but decided that some token effort was in order to honor the day. Or Mollie, at least. A clean face was easy. As long as he didn't have to go deeper than skimming the surface.

He had boundaries. No disrespect to his temporary hostess and benefactor, but he would not be railroaded into attending church. He'd gladly unplug her sink drain, haul boxes downstairs, cut a Christmas tree—even paint rooms that didn't need it—but he drew the line at being herded into a pew.

In fact, he was surprised that Mollie hadn't argued with him or tried her usual ploy of spinning refusal into agreement. Breanna had been as equally astonished, and he chuckled remembering her near choking incident at the table. Her soft gray eyes had increased in size as she stared over her napkin.

Mollie played her cards close to her apron, and this morning she'd been as pleasant as ever with a quick breakfast of orange juice and sausage biscuits. Hand-pressed sausage and homemade biscuits, of course. Fast-food joints were quickly fading from his list of places to eat.

The muffled thud of two car doors announced the women's return from church. He snagged his coat from the rocker in his room and checked the pockets for work gloves. Nada. He'd have to swing by the ranch on the way out.

He trotted down the stairs as the grandfather clock in the hall struck the three-quarter hour.

Mollie came through the front door, followed by Breanna dressed in jeans and snow boots.

"I just have to get my heavy coat and gloves, and we can go," she said. The morning cold had flushed her cheeks and lips.

Not that he noticed.

"I'll go warm up the truck." He pulled on his jacket and zipped it.

"Wait a minute, Matthew," Mollie called from the kitchen.

He stopped in front of the door.

Mollie hurried back still wearing her wool coat and scarf and carrying a basket.

"Isn't it a little cold for a picnic," he said with a teasing grin.

"Not a picnic." She shoved the basket toward him. "This is the easiest way to carry a thermos of hot cocoa and a care-package. I imagine you'll stop for a meal along the way, but this will be a nice snack on the road." She patted his arm. "And you'll need a little extra something for chopping down that perfect tree."

"Thanks, Mollie. We'll make good use of it." He suppressed a sudden urge to give her a peck on her grandmotherly cheek.

She reached up and patted his face with a gloved hand. "You have a good time." Then she lowered her voice and stretched closer to him. "Take your time coming home. I'll have something warming in the oven if you're still hungry when you get here."

Guess a kiss would have been in order. "You're spoiling me, Mollie Murphy. How am I ever supposed to survive as an independent bachelor?"

She looked him square in the eye. "You're not."

"Ready." Breanna appeared in an ice-blue parka with white fur edging the hood. The contrast against her dark hair was striking.

"So am I." He hefted the basket. "Never got around to warming the truck, but Mollie's sending us off with hot chocolate."

Breanna helped her grandmother out of her coat and hung it on the bentwood hall tree before giving her a hug. "Thanks, Mollie. You're the best."

"I know, dear. You just make sure to get the best tree." She waved over her shoulder at them on her way to the kitchen. "Have fun."

Breanna dashed down the porch steps and up to the passenger door to find it locked. Matt grinned at her through the window as he opened his side, set the basket on the seat, and pushed the lock release. By then she was jumping up and down from the cold with her hands buried in her coat pockets.

"What are you going to do at eight thousand feet if you're freezing now?" He started the engine and cranked the heater to its highest setting.

"I'm getting my circulation going." She turned her face to him, and her eyes sparkled as she stomped her feet on the floorboard. She hunched her shoulders and burrowed deeper into her parka. "It's colder in here than it is outside."

"A balmy thirty-one degrees out there," he said, checking the outdoor temperature reading on the dashboard. "Heat wave."

The sound of her laughter stirred something in him as they drove out of town. But when he pulled into his long, snowy lane instead of heading straight for the Interstate, she gave him a guarded look.

"Need my work gloves. It'll only take a second. I'll leave the engine running for you."

~

The Oxford place appeared much the same as it had when Breanna left for college. The front porch on the house sagged pathetically and one corner post was missing. Snow covered the lawn, but a clear path stretched from the driveway to the front door and another to the big barn.

Past the end of the house, corrals leaned wearily against one side of the barn, a few cross rails missing, but a brown horse stood unbothered by neither its accommodations nor the weather. Its breath puffed white around its muzzle, and its ears pricked toward the house. Must be Matt's. Regardless, the cowboy-architect certainly had his manual labor cut out for him in this fixer-upper.

She unzipped her parka, pulled off her gloves, and stuffed them in her pockets. The cab's cozy interior smelled like pumpkin bread and her stomach rumbled. Tempted to dig into Mollie's provisions, she peeked into the basket but put the lid down and waited. She didn't want to look piggish.

Why should she care what Matt Dawson thought? She sighed and instead considered the countryside. Only in Colorado could the sky be that blue—clear, cold, and cerulean over frosted peaks to the west. Aaron was probably missing it. Again. No doubt he was pushing iron around at the gym or slumped on his sofa playing video games. Why had she ever thought they shared anything in common?

The solid thud of the front door brought her attention back to the moment. Matt held up leather work gloves. Aaron probably didn't even own a pair.

"Did you leave anything for me to eat?" Matt tossed the gloves on the dashboard, took his place behind the wheel, and unzipped his jacket.

"What makes you think I'd eat while you were gone?" Her stomach rumbled again and she hoped he couldn't hear it.

"Because I'm starving, and I figured you would be, too. I remember what you said about third graders."

She detected a tease behind the quirk of his mouth. "I am not a third grader."

His husky laugh made her arms tingle. "But since you mentioned it, I'll serve while you drive."

"Thatta girl."

The off-handed remark worried her. What did she know about this guy? Here she sat heading up the interstate with a near stranger, pushed into his company by her grandmother who loaded them with treats for the trip. Trouble was, she trusted Mollie's judgment. The woman was rarely wrong where people were concerned.

Oh Lord, keep me safe today. Help me pay attention to what's going on.

When it came to Mollie's judgment on food, she was *never* wrong. Breanna unscrewed the top of a large thermos and the aroma of hot cocoa swirled into her face. She filled one travel mug for Matt, secured the top and handed it to him. He took it with a smile as honest as the cloudless day, and her heart hummed an unfamiliar note.

She filled the second travel mug for herself and set the thermos in its corner between two sliced loaves of plastic-wrapped bread. "Pumpkin or cranberry nut?"

Matt glanced into the basket that filled the seat between them. "Pumpkin, of course."

Breanna unwrapped the darker loaf and handed him a thick slice on a red paper napkin. "Mollie thinks of everything."

"She sure does. But honestly," he gave her a serious look and nodded at the basket, "I expected her to pack china teacups and saucers in there."

Breanna laughed and bit into her own slice. "Your truck isn't the boarding house. She must have made an exception."

Little traffic hindered them on the trip up I-25, and easy conversation about Mollie and teaching and architectural design made the three-hour journey feel like her usual twenty-minute drive to school. By half past one, they were on a dirt road headed toward a green Forest Service truck parked next to a gated fence. A ranger exited the pickup as they approached.

Matt stopped at the gate and rolled down his window. "Good afternoon." He laid his right arm across the top of the steering wheel.

"You're here to cut a tree, right?" The ranger nodded at Breanna and returned his attention to Matt.

"Yes sir. Ten dollars?"

"Per tree." He exchanged Matt's $10 bill for a receipt and tugged on his green cap. "You just made it. No entry after two thirty since you have to be out by four."

Matt looked toward the forest. "How far in do we need to go?"

The ranger followed his gaze. "Not far. You can cut anywhere beyond this fence line." He slapped the top of the cab. "Good luck and watch the time."

"Thanks. We will."

Matt rolled up the window, shifted into four-wheel drive and pulled through the gate. "Here we go."

"That's a lot to choose from." Breanna frowned toward the dense forest sweeping up the mountain like a dark mantle.

"Do you know what you want exactly? How big?"

"I don't think we need anything over six feet." She sized him up. "How tall are you?"

"Six-two."

"Perfect."

He grinned at her quick reply, and she sensed a witty retort approaching.

"Thank you. I like to think so myself."

She rolled her eyes. "You have more in common with third-grade boys than you think."

He tossed her a wounded look and clutched at his chest.

"You'll get over it," she said. "They always do."

A sudden bump bounced her against her seatbelt, and she grabbed for the armrest.

"Hang on," Matt said. "It will probably get worse before it gets better."

The forest closed in around them, the road roughened, and the depth of snow increased as they climbed the mountain.

"Want to try around here?"

"Sure." Breanna slipped her gloves on, zipped her parka, and pulled up the hood. "This is as good a place as any."

Ahead, another pickup sat off the road as far as possible and Matt pulled in behind it.

A thin crust topped the snow, but still they sank into it up to their knees when they stepped out. Matt opened his truck tool box and pulled out a saw and rope. He handed the rope to Breanna and pulled on his work gloves. "Lead the way."

She stared at him, surprised that he didn't march off into the woods with a manly "follow me" attitude. Another note in that unfamiliar melody sounded in her heart.

Trudging through the knee-deep snowpack was harder than she remembered. "I'd forgotten how difficult this is," she said, slightly out of breath.

"Don't you do this every year?" Matt's longer strides had moved him beside her as they walked.

"Actually, I haven't done this since I was a kid. After Jim passed away, Mollie and I always went to the local Christmas tree lot."

He stopped in his tracks, and she looked over her shoulder. "What?"

"You mean this isn't an annual tradition?"

"It was." She faced him. "But not for the past twelve years or so."

Unspoken thoughts bunched on his face. Anger or amusement, she wasn't sure.

"You know what's going on, don't you?" he asked.

Heat rose to her cheeks, and she wished it would sink to her snow-entombed toes instead.

"Yes, I do." She scanned the forest that cloaked them. "But how do you tell Mollie no?"

His lighthearted laugh relieved her. "You don't mind?"

She didn't mind at all, though she had resented Mollie's maneuverings at first. Matt was easy to be around, talk to, and laugh with. But she couldn't tell him that.

"Like I said before, I'm used to third graders." She turned to continue hiking, and from the corner of her eye saw him reach for the snow. She ducked just in time.

"Hey! What was that for?" She tried to escape but fell instead and landed on her backside.

He scooped another handful, and she did the same. The dry snow failed to stick together or land with much force, and they managed only to cover each other with fine powder and laughter.

"Peace!" Breanna floundered from her fallen position and struggled to get to her feet.

In two long strides, he was beside her and offered his free hand. "Peace."

He pulled her up as lightly as if she weighed nothing at all, and she put her other hand out to keep from falling against him as she regained her balance. "Tree, Mr. Dawson. We need a tree."

He held her gloved hand a moment longer, as if measuring its weight in his own.

Breaking their gaze she peered into the woods again. "I can't see the tree for the forest."

Laughing, he stepped around her and into the lead. "Don't you have that backward, Madam School Teacher?"

"On purpose. Look at all these magnificent spruces and pines. Which one is the perfect choice?"

"That's your job. I'm just the hired help." He raised the small hand saw in demonstration and took off into the snow.

Breanna followed, grateful to have his deep footprints to tread in rather than trying to blaze the trail herself. She appraised the trees as they walked and after a few strides chose one off to the left.

"What about that one over there?" She stopped and pointed to a stately blue spruce grouped with several other shorter trees.

Matt tramped over and pushed snow away from the tree's lower branches. Then he wrapped a hand around the base. "Has to be smaller than six inches around. This one will work."

"Stand next to it."

He obliged, grinning next to the slightly taller tree.

Perfect.

"We can't leave more than a six-inch stump," he said, "so it'll be only a little shorter once we set it up in the dining room."

"Perfect."

He grinned wider, if possible.

"The tree, Mr. Dawson. The tree." She answered his grin with one of her own and helped him scoop away the snow so he'd have a clear cutting zone.

Chapter Five

Wrapped in tarp and secured with rope, the spruce lay cocooned in the bed of the truck. Matt rechecked the ropes on each side and walked around to the driver's door. Breanna had already settled in and was pouring more cocoa into his mug. He could get used to this. To her. He'd better snag that thought before he got tangled.

With no room to turn around, he backed most of the way out until they reached a wide curve in the road. From the deepening shadows around them, it had to be close to four. He checked the clock on the dash—three forty-nine. They'd cut it close. That little snowball fight on the way in probably cost them a few minutes, but it was worth it.

He took a drink of lukewarm cocoa and eyed the picnic basket. Breanna noticed.

"Bread or cookies?" she said as she lifted the lid. "Both?"

She snickered under her breath and opened one of the red napkins, filling it with a frosted

Christmas tree, a chocolate chip cookie, and two slices of pumpkin bread.

"Thanks." He laid the offering on the narrow strip of seat between his right leg and the basket and stole a glance at her face. Peaceful. Happy. So unlike what he'd grown up with.

The ranger at the gate waved them through and park-like grassland opened around them. Late afternoon shadows stretched across the road, and the sun hesitated just above the mountains. He figured a half hour of daylight remained.

"Where do you want to eat dinner?"

She pushed her hood back and static drew out the shorter lengths of her hair like a science experiment. She tried to smooth it down but failed, and it made him smile.

"You're laughing at me."

"No, I'm not. I'm smiling. There's a big difference."

"There's a big difference in your hair, too. This isn't fair." She tried again to flatten the static-empowered strays and ended by retrieving a band from her pocket and twisting it around the longer hair.

"Sorry. But unless you want me to douse you with warm cocoa, there's not much I can do to help your fly-away look."

She shot him a warning and licked her palm before running it over her head.

He stifled a belly laugh at her obvious frustration and focused on the window. Lights were flickering on in ranch houses and highway signs glowed against the falling darkness. "Want to stop in Fort Collins, Loveland, or go all the way?"

She glared at him.

"Home." He choked in spite of himself. "All the way home. To the Berthoud Boarding House. To Mollie."

Obviously embarrassed, she stared straight ahead. "If you don't mind, I'd like to stop. Breakfast and cookies aren't enough for me after all that exertion today."

He snorted. "Exertion? Who cut the tree and dragged it out?"

"And who had to defend herself from assault in a less-than-superior position on her backside in the snow?"

He caught the playful taunt in her voice and nodded in agreement. "You've got me there."

He tracked a passing road sign with several restaurant logos. "So what's your pleasure? Chicken, tacos, noodles, or steak?"

"Chicken. Unless you prefer steak."

"Are you kidding? Of course I prefer steak. Chicken it is."

"How chivalrous of you."

"You're welcome."

~

The hot food warmed Matt from the inside out, and Breanna's company made it even better. Most nights he ate alone.

"So tell me about yourself." She eyed him over her coffee.

"What's to tell? I'm a roper, freelance architect, and wannabe carpenter renovating the Oxford place."

She set down her cup and grabbed a piece of chicken. "Tell me about growing up. You know about my childhood. I'm sure Mollie filled you in on all the glorious details."

He knew this would happen. He took a deep breath, scooped in a mouthful of mashed potatoes and gravy, and swallowed. "My mom was an alcoholic." Might as well shoot straight with the teacher. She'd probably heard it all before.

Her expression softened as she waited for him to elaborate.

"No dad in the picture. Mom worked when she was sober, but we lived on welfare most of the time, and charity from a nearby church. I wanted my life to be different, and after high school I moved in with a buddy. Got an associate degree at the local junior college and my grades earned me a scholarship to UC Boulder. Mom died before I graduated."

She fingered her napkin. "I'm sorry."

"Not your fault."

"I know, but I'm still sorry. It sounds like you didn't have much of a family life."

He finished off his potatoes and picked up his coffee. "Nada."

"A lot of kids have a similar story. Most of my students come from single-parent homes or blended families. Some of them have a strong core unit, but many of them don't."

He noticed a subtle change in her tone.

"You'd be an inspiration to them," she said.

"Me? Why?"

She leaned forward on her elbows. "Because you persevered. You didn't quit, and you made a life for yourself."

He glanced at the chicken bones on his plate. "The church I mentioned helped in that department. A youth leader there kept a tight rein on me. As much as he could."

For the first time, her face registered surprise. "So why the strong objection to going with Mollie and me today?"

Her question cut closer than his morning shave. He didn't want to go that deep, but he felt the layers falling away beneath the smooth edge of her sincerity.

"My mom was a hypocrite. She'd go to church on Sunday morning, sing at the top of her voice, repent and cry, and drink herself stupid that night." He looked across the table into compassionate eyes. "It sickened me."

"But the youth leader hung on."

"Yeah, he did. He was the closest thing I had to a father." He drained his coffee, set the cup in his plate, and scooted to the open end of the booth seat.

"All of us have a little hypocrite hiding inside," she said softly. "What better place to go when you're hurting and need help than to God?"

The bare truth of her quiet statement hit him in the chest, and he felt the first discomfort of the day. "Time to go."

Disappointment colored her voice. "You're right. We don't want Mollie to worry about us."

He took their plates to the trash and recalled the woman's parting message about keeping dinner warm for them. She'd shown him more motherly attention in a week than his own mother ever had.

~

His full disclosure clouded the space between them, and Breanna blamed herself. They drove through the night in silence, testimony that he hadn't appreciated her interrogation. She'd obviously pulled a scab off a still-tender wound.

An overhead highway sign announced nine miles until the Berthoud exit, and she thought back over the day they'd spent. Until dinner, she'd had more fun than she'd ever had with Aaron.

The truck's headlights caught an unfamiliar shape on the shoulder, and she looked closer as they sped by. "Did you see that? It might have been a dog."

"Probably a coyote," Matt said without slowing his speed.

"No, really. I think it was a dog. Can't we go back? It could be hit out here on the highway."

He looked at her as if she'd lost her mind, but she didn't care. "Please."

He took his foot off the accelerator, flipped on his right signal, and slowed to a stop on the shoulder. "You sure about this?"

"Yes. What if it's lost? Or abandoned?"

He shoved the truck into reverse and stretched his right arm across the seat as he slowly backed up. "I don't see it. Probably took off."

"Keep going. A little farther." She twisted around in her seat and peered into the dark, praying the animal hadn't run into traffic and been hit. "There!"

He braked to a slow stop and put the truck in park.

"He's limping. Oh, Matt, I think he's hurt." She unfastened her seatbelt and reached for the door handle.

"Hang on a minute." He laid a hand on her shoulder. "You can't go out there. It could be mean or rabid."

She dared him with an arched eyebrow. "I'm going. You coming?"

He muttered something under his breath. "Hold on. Let me go first."

The skinny dog limped along the edge of the roadway, head drooping. When they stepped out of the pickup, it stopped and lifted its head.

Matt cut in front of her and stooped down. "Come on boy. You okay?"

The gangly animal wagged its tail but didn't move.

"See, it's friendly," Breanna said.

He held his arm out to block her approach. "Give me a second here." He inched closer, still stooped, but angled away, leading with his right side. "Come on fella. We're not going to hurt you."

The dog lowered its head and whined. The tail continued to wag.

Close enough to touch, Matt reached into his pocket for a work glove and slipped it on. He held his hand out for the dog to sniff, fingers down.

The animal nosed his palm and whimpered, then dropped to the pavement.

Matt stroked the scruffy head and scooted closer, reaching back along the emaciated body.

"Oh, Matt, he's so thin. He must be starving." Breanna knelt on the off-road side, and following Matt's lead, offered the scent of own gloved hands. The thin tail thumped the ground and a deep moan emanated from its throat. Breanna's eyes teared as she rubbed along the bony back, feeling every rib.

"We have to take him home." She silently pleaded with him to agree and saw the moment he relented. "Thank you," she whispered, laying a hand on his arm. Her breath formed a white cloud between them.

"I'm going to pick you up, boy." The dog released a long sigh as Matt's soothing voice intoned around it. Bending lower, he cradled the dog.

Breanna ran to open the passenger door.

Laying the dog on the floor, Matt gently pulled his arms away. She climbed onto the seat and traded places with the basket, settling her feet on the floor at the dog's head. It whimpered and raised its nose to her boots with the quick flick of a pink tongue.

Matt slid in behind the wheel and shut the door. He shook his head as he fastened his seatbelt and looked at her. "You're really something, you know that?"

Glad it was dark so he couldn't see her wet lashes, she leaned over. "He's grateful. You can see it in his eyes."

"Put on your seatbelt." Matt pulled a retracted belt from the center of the bench seat while she felt for the other half.

His hand covered hers as she connected the two halves, and a warm tingle traveled through her arms and into her shoulders. "Thank you for stopping. You're my hero."

They drove the remaining few miles in silence, and each time she leaned over the dog it thumped its tail as if it knew she cared. What would Mollie say when they came through the door with this bag of bones?

As a child, Breanna once brought home a stray kitten, and her grandmother heated milk and made a bed on the back porch. Would she respond in kind to a mongrel they'd found limping along the highway?

~

Matt had been called a few choice names in his life aside from the recent Scrooge incident, but never "hero." His chest tightened at the memory of Breanna's soft voice and shining eyes. He knew she'd shed a few tears, but they were for that mutt on the floor, not his acquiescence to her request. Did it matter?

Yes.

The porch light welcomed them home and a dim glow from the back of the house said Mollie was waiting in the kitchen. He hoped for Breanna's sake the woman welcomed the dog as easily as she'd welcomed him in his hour of need.

"Go open the door, and I'll carry him in."

Breanna scooted out the driver's side behind him and reached for the picnic basket. Then she laid a hand on his chest and paused. "Again, thank you."

The light touch of her fingers sucked the breath out of him and he pushed away the temptation to lean down and kiss her. "You're welcome."

When they opened the front door, "In the kitchen" floated down the hallway. Matt attempted a deep breath as he approached the warm, cheerful room.

"We brought something besides a tree," he said, his arms full of matted hair and sagging skin.

The dog raised its ragged head and looked at Mollie, pumping its tail in a feeble hello.

"Oh, you poor dear." Both hands flew to her cheeks, and she rushed across the kitchen. "Just look at you." She narrowed her eyes at Matt. "Did you hit him?"

He huffed out a relieved chuckle. "No. Your granddaughter here didn't want to leave him limping along the Interstate, so of course we went back and picked him up."

Breanna was already in the enclosed back porch making a bed out of old blankets. "Bring him out here," she called.

"I'll get him some water and a few pieces of left-over roast." Mollie dug an aluminum dish out of her drawer of odd pots and pans and filled it with cool water. Then she pulled the roast from the oven and cut off a few bite-sized pieces. "I don't think he's eaten in quite some time. We don't want to give him too much and make him sick." She dropped the pieces into a china soup bowl and followed Matt out to the porch.

When Matt saw the good bowl in her hands, he cocked an eyebrow.

"He's a guest." She set the bowl close to the blankets. "I do have a dishwasher you know."

The three of them watched the dog inhale the tender bits of meat, cough a couple of times, and then lick its jowls. It looked at them as if to say thank you. Then it drank slowly from the aluminum bowl. With one more grateful glance, it laid its big head on its front paws and sighed with contentment.

"You are very welcome," Mollie said and returned to the kitchen.

Matt and Breanna followed, and she closed the door, looking through the glass pane at the peaceful dog. "What shall we call him?"

"Rover?" he said.

"No."

"Butch?"

"No!"

"How 'bout Roady?"

Breanna gave him a puzzled look. "Like people who follow their favorite band around, helping them set up?"

"Yeah. Sort of." Matt rubbed the side of his head and took a seat at the kitchen table. "Why not? We did find him on the road."

"Well, he didn't set anything up, but I guess it'll do."

"Don't be so sure," Mollie mumbled.

Matt caught a sly smile on the woman's kind face.

"I think you should take Roady to the vet tomorrow." Mollie untied her apron and hung it over a chair. "Make sure he doesn't have the mange, get his teeth checked, and see if he needs any shots. A crippled house guest is one thing, but a mangy critter is quite another."

Breanna pulled her grandmother into a hug. "Does this mean we can keep him?"

Mollie returned the affectionate squeeze. "If someone doesn't come looking for him, yes. But you should run an ad all the same, just to be sure."

"Thanks, Mollie." Breanna planted a kiss on each rosy cheek. "That's what we did for the kitten, remember? How long did we wait for someone to come for it?"

Mollie pattered into the hall and called back. "About ten years, if my memory serves me. Good night, you two. Put the roast away before you turn in. I'm going to bed."

Breanna giggled and joined Matt at the table, happier than he'd seen her in the last two days. "You hungry?"

He shook his head. "No, believe it or not. I just need a hot shower after all the tree lugging and dog carrying. Especially the tree lugging."

She smiled across the short distance. "You go ahead, and I'll unpack the basket."

Why hadn't her boyfriend come with her? What an idiot.

He forced himself to keep his grimy hands from reaching across the table. "Sure you don't need my help?"

She stood and her eyes sparkled with silent laughter. "Scoot," she said, mimicking Mollie's hand flutter. Her gaze swept the length of his coat. "If you have another jacket, leave that one by the front door, and I'll take it to the cleaners tomorrow. Go on, now."

"Yes, ma'am." He slipped his coat off. "You're as bossy as your grandmother."

"I've had lots of practice."

"I know. I know," he said as he headed for the hall. "Third-graders."

Chapter Six

The delicious promise of homemade waffles teased from the hallway, pulling Breanna out of bed, into her clothes, and straight to the kitchen.

"Good morning, dear. Did you sleep well?"

"Like a stone, as always." She gave her grandmother a quick hug from behind and then went to the porch door to check on their newest house guest. Roast and waffle bits disappeared beneath Roady's snout. "You're spoiling him, you know."

"Not possible. That poor thing hasn't eaten well since I don't know when."

Breanna noticed a syrupy plate in the sink and the sight plucked a note of disappointment. "Did Matt already eat and leave?"

"Yes, he's long gone. Wanted to check on things at his place but he did get the tree up." Mollie turned from her post at the waffle iron. "Did you see it? It's lovely."

Breanna went to the dining room entry and surveyed the stately spruce in the corner. Even from the doorway she detected its fresh scent. The perfume stirred images of her day with Matt. "You're right. It is lovely. Even without decorations."

"I knew you'd find the perfect tree." Mollie lifted a similarly perfect waffle from the iron and laid it on a flower-edged china plate. "If only you had such taste in men," she mumbled under her breath.

"What was that?" Breanna took the plate and sat at the table where she spread butter across the waffle squares and filled each one with thick, amber syrup.

"I said you have good taste in trees." Mollie brought another plate and joined her.

Breanna shot an accusing glance across the table. "Uh-huh."

"I've been doing a little research this morning." Mollie glazed her own waffle. "That mongrel out there looks to be part Airedale. Did you know they shed their entire coat twice a year?"

Breanna wasn't surprised by her grandmother's newfound knowledge. Although old-fashioned, Mollie was quite adept at Googling anything she needed to learn.

"Part?"

"His tail's not quite right for a purebred."

"So you're an expert now?" She giggled at her grandmother's air of authority. "Well, his teeth must be in good condition. He's made short work of all your snacks."

"They still need to be checked. And on your way home from the vet, get some dry dog food and one of those nice big beds. He'll need something a little better than old blankets this winter."

Breanna hid her grin behind her coffee-filled teacup. Roady obviously had a new fan. "Aren't you going to help me get him to the vet?"

"Oh, no. Matthew will be back this morning to take him in the truck. He assured me of that before he left."

Tiny flares tingled down Breanna's arms and into her fingertips.

Mollie studied her. "Do you consider that good news?"

Defenses heightened. "Why would I consider it good news?"

"You're evading my question."

Breanna sighed. She didn't want to go there with her grandmother. She hadn't gone there with herself. "You're doing it again, Mollie Matchmaker." She gathered her dishes and took them to the sink.

Mollie swept away the words with a hand. "I'm doing no such thing. Matthew is a nice young man. So much more well-rounded than that self-absorbed thing you brought with you last summer. Couldn't even stay more than a few days. Had to dash back to Greeley for whatever reason."

Breanna recalled her disappointment at Aaron's restlessness. He'd said he felt he didn't live up to Mollie's expectations—and he'd been right. She should have paid more attention to her grandmother's intuition and kicked him to the curb before school started.

The front door opened. "In the kitchen," Molly called before Breanna could check the hallway.

The sound of footsteps in the hall kicked up her pulse in anticipation of seeing the cowboy-architect-tree-cutter, and she grabbed her cup from the sink. More coffee suddenly seemed like a good idea.

He filled the doorway like a vision of Paul Bunyan in faded jeans, work boots, and a plaid flannel shirt. Biting her tongue, she refrained from asking if Babe the Blue Ox waited outside.

"I brought something for Roady." He held up a blue collar and matching leash.

Like embers beneath a warm breath, the earlier sparks flared to life. "Did you just happen to have those at your old, cold house?"

He grinned and the dimple winked through a day-old beard. "Not exactly."

"It's perfect, Matthew. How thoughtful." Mollie patted him on the shoulder. "Why don't you try it on him? Maybe if you get to the vet's early, you won't have to wait for an appointment."

So much for coffee. Breanna returned her cup to the sink and joined Matt on the back porch. Roady sat patiently as Matt fastened the collar around the scrawny neck. The long tail thumped the floor.

"He likes it," she said.

"Makes him feel like he belongs." Matt attached the leash and tugged. Roady readily followed him into the kitchen.

I know the feeling.

Breanna thought of the day Mollie and Jim led her into her very own room. And the day they showed her the legal document that officially made her a Murphy.

Her throat tightened as she choked down the emotions. "I'll get my jacket and meet you at the truck."

"Don't forget those other things I mentioned, dear." Mollie pulled some folded bills from her apron pocket. "This should cover everything."

"Nothing doing." Breanna took the money and gently tucked it back in the oversized pocket. "I've got this." She kissed Mollie's cheek. "I'm also stopping by the dry cleaners. Do you have anything you want me to take?"

"No, but if I think of anything, I'll call."

The click-clack of doggy toenails punctuated Matt's steps behind her, and she paused in the entryway to grab his jacket.

"I'll hold his leash if you'll warm up the truck."

"Already warm and waiting," he said as he opened the door and extended a gallant hand.

A trail of exhaust puffed from the back of his pickup, and she nodded. "Good job, Mr. Dawson."

"Anything for the school teacher."

She led them out the door and across the lawn and scooted to the center of the bench seat. "Here, boy, come up here with us."

Still weak, the dog put one paw on the floor board and raised doleful eyes to Matt.

"All right, fella. Here we go." With a gentle lift, he boosted the animal into the cab where it lay on the floor and thumped its tail.

Matt walked around to the driver's side. Breanna laid his parka on the seat beside her and buckled the center belt across her lap.

"Thank you for keeping the truck warm. I think Roady appreciates it, too."

"It's brisk this morning, but not as cold as it was inside that old farmhouse." He belted himself in, checked the side mirror, and pulled into the street. "After the vet, the cleaners, and whatever other errands Mollie has for you, we'll stop by the appliance store and check on my furnace."

And if it's in you'll go home. The thought dulled Breanna's excitement. Without a furnace, Matt was bound to the Berthoud Boarding House. As soon as it arrived and he installed it, he'd go home. Where he belonged.

"I'm new to the area, so you'll have to choose the vet. Where do I go from here?"

"Let's try the Schaffer Veterinary Clinic. Take a left at the stoplight."

~

In the last forty-eight hours, Matt had served more domestic duty than he had since leaving home as a teenager. Living alone the past five years, he'd missed out on a lot, and the thought of trading in bachelorhood for a partnership raised appealing possibilities. He glanced toward Breanna and the ugly dog at her feet. Considering the obvious contrast in his passengers, he chuckled to himself.

"What's so funny?"

Oh-oh. Should he take the chance? He flipped his signal and turned left at the intersection.

"Don't take this the wrong way, but I just realized I've got a beauty and a beast with me this morning."

Breanna sniffed a half-laugh. "I guess it depends on who's who."

He shot her a questioning look.

"So?" She lifted her chin. "Who's who?"

It was make or break now. "Roady's the beast, of course. That makes you the beauty."

He checked to see her reaction and noted a soft flush on her cheeks.

She leaned over and rubbed Roady behind the ears. "You poor thing. He thinks you're a beast."

Matt exhaled a nervous breath. "Well, unless you'd rather—"

"Don't even think it."

He laughed out loud, relieved that she'd played along with him.

"So Roady." She lifted his muzzle and looked in the dog's eyes. "If I say I love you, will you become a handsome prince?"

Now it was Matt's turn to feel the heat rush to his face. He'd trade places with that mutt in a heartbeat.

~

The vet gave Matt a bottle of medicated shampoo and recommended a specific brand of dog food until Roady fully recovered. He treated broken blisters on the dog's foot pads, vaccinated him for rabies, checked his teeth, and sent them on their way. Roady was one tough mongrel.

Back in the pickup, Matt thought Roady looked happier.

"So what's on your list there, Beauty?"

Breanna frowned as she reached into her jacket pocket. "I hope that's not going to become a habit." She unfolded a small paper. "Unless you want me to start calling *you* beast."

He considered a couple of clever responses she probably wouldn't think were so clever. "If you insist."

"I do."

Another remark popped into his head at her clipped reply, and he clamped his teeth together.

"Dog food. Dog bed. Cleaners." She refolded the note and tucked it in her pocket. "Furnace."

The last word carried a different tone. Disappointment?

He stayed in the truck with Roady while Breanna picked out what they needed from a super mart. He stayed in the truck at the cleaners, too. And just for the heck of it, he stayed in the outside lane as they passed the appliance store on the way home.

When he pulled up to the boarding house, a worried Mollie opened the front door.

Puzzled, he went around to help Roady out of the truck, gave Breanna the leash, and grabbed the dog food and over-sized, green plaid dog bed.

"Mollie," Breanna asked as they stepped inside. "What's wrong?"

Matt left the two women alone and headed for the back porch. The lines creasing Mollie's usually smooth forehead told him something was up.

Chapter Seven

Breanna hadn't seen her grandmother this concerned since last summer's hail storm destroyed her flower garden. "Are you okay?"

Mollie folded her hands at her waist and frowned. "I have two more guests coming in this weekend."

Breanna sighed in relief but tried not to discredit her grandmother's obvious discomfort. "Isn't that all right? This *is* a boarding house."

"Tiffany Collins and her friend." She searched Breanna's face as if waiting for a reply.

"All right." Breanna mentally filed through the faces of her co-workers, people she knew from church in Greeley, and parents she'd met at conferences. "Should I know the name?"

"Her friend is Aaron Reynolds."

That name hit her like a blow to the chest.

"I'm so sorry, Bre. It didn't register with me until after Tiffany hung up." Mollie rubbed her temple and pushed back a loose strand of white. "I guess I'm getting old."

Breanna dropped Roady's leash and reached for her grandmother's hands. "You're not getting old, Mollie. You run a boarding house. You're not required to remember the names of everyone I know."

The woman's shoulders drooped. "I can call her and tell her I made a mistake—that I don't have any rooms available."

The temptation tasted like revenge, but Breanna couldn't let her grandmother do that. It went against everything they believed in. And Mollie needed the income. She squeezed the capable hands. "We'll get through this—they won't be here forever." She hoped. "When do they arrive?"

"Friday night. Tiffany said they'd be leaving Sunday morning to go skiing at Copper Mountain."

Breanna pulled the troubled woman into her arms. "I can't believe he did this. He knows this is your boarding house." Aaron was supposed to come with *her,* not someone else. She blinked away the bitterness threatening to surface. She refused to make this worse for Mollie.

"He doesn't know, dear."

Breanna held her grandmother at arm's length and looked into her sweet face. "What do you mean?"

"Tiffany told me she planned to surprise him."

Some surprise. "Well, I think it's going to be a doozie." She rubbed Mollie's upper arms with both hands. "A weekend is cake. We'll be fine. They'll be gone before Christmas Eve, and it will be just the three of us again."

Where did that come from?

"And we still have a few days to bake and paint before they arrive." Suddenly the thought of Aaron and Miss Dumbbell sleeping in paint-fumy rooms cheered her. She'd have to repent.

At her feet, Roady whimpered and looked down the hall.

"Okay, Beast. Come on. Let's get you something to eat and introduce you to your fancy new bed."

"Beast?" Mollie fussed with the sash of her apron and turned toward the kitchen. "I thought you named him Roady."

"We did. Long story." One that Breanna hoped had many more chapters. She wrapped an arm around her grandmother's shoulders. If Aaron didn't spoil things.

~

Breanna tried to make up for Mollie's quieter mood at dinner in the kitchen that evening and reminded her of their plans to decorate the tree.

"And I'll get those boxes upstairs so we can eat in the dining room again," Matt added.

Breanna watched the muscles in his face as he spoke, the way the dimple appeared and disappeared, the way the light played in his dark eyes. He seemed like part of the family—someone always available to lend a hand. Someone to be there. To laugh with. She'd never thought of Aaron like that, and the thought of Aaron sharing the same table and roof made her nauseous.

What if Matt left?

She listened as he did his best to engage Mollie in an argument about Roady's ancestry. His eyes twinkled and that parenthesis deepened when he tried to keep from smiling. He caught Breanna watching him, and she looked away, her face flooding in hot misery. His deep throaty chuckle sent shivers up her back.

Tonight, after the tree, she'd tell him about Aaron. Could he have overheard her conversation with Mollie? Did he already know?

Oh Lord, please don't let it make him leave.

~

Christmas music floated out from Mollie's office computer and mingled with the mulled cider warming on the stove. Breanna knelt among the boxes and cartons of ornaments, unwrapping delicate glass bulbs and whimsical shapes.

"Some of these hung on Mollie's family's tree when she was a child." She held out an angel with spun glass hair. "But this one she gave to me the first Christmas I spent here."

The concern on Matt's face amused her. "Don't worry. You're not going to break it."

"Is it that obvious?" His hand dwarfed the heavenly messenger.

Breanna shook her head. "You're doing fine. I appreciate you helping me at all, especially on the higher branches. I always had to stand on a chair."

He suspended the angel near the top of the tree.

"When we get the top third finished, I'll let you off the hook. No pun intended."

He groaned and rubbed his hands down his face. "Surely someone with your educational background can do better than that."

She grinned at him and placed a large crystal snowflake in his open palm. "You don't have to help with the whole tree. You can go chop wood or do some other manly chore."

Matt hung the snowflake, studied it for a moment, and moved it to a different branch. Then he knelt beside her. "I'm enjoying this," he said with surprising softness.

Breanna took a deep breath hoping to ward off the rising crimson tide and dug into another carton of ornaments. "I'm glad." She pawed through the tissue. "Did you help your mother do this when you were a kid?"

A shadow crossed his features.

Oops. None of my business.

Whatever it was vanished when he met her eyes. "No. We didn't do this. Christmas wasn't exactly a family event. But I helped decorate the tree at the church a couple of years. That youth leader I mentioned did his best to keep me involved."

Grateful for his openness, Breanna's heart squeezed at the thought of what his childhood must have been. So unlike hers.

The tissue-wrapped bundle she'd chosen held a miniature Paul Bunyan with an ax resting against his shoulder. She smoothed the little man's shirt and handed it over to the life-size version.

"Is this one special?" He suspended the legendary lumberjack between his thumb and forefinger and searched her face.

"Mollie gave this to Jim one year because he always cut our Christmas tree." She pulled another wad of tissue out of the box.

"And?"

He didn't miss much. Still stooped with one knee on the floor, he waited.

She relented with a nervous sigh. "He reminds me of you. You looked almost exactly like that this morning when you came in with Roady's new collar and leash."

He held the ornament at arm's length and turned it around. "Not exactly."

His tone suggested grave consideration, but she caught the dimple.

"No leash. And the ax is all wrong. I used a hand saw."

She appreciated his playfulness—until he hung Paul Bunyan right next to the flaxen-haired angel.

Her pulse quickened, and she refocused on the box. Only three days, and already he held her heart like a delicate ornament of handspun glass.

"Cider, anyone?" Mollie broke the tension as she bustled in with a silver tea tray and service for three. "Oh, it's coming along nicely. How kind of you, Matthew, to give us a hand. A *tall* hand, I might say." She set the china cups and saucers on the table and squeezed into the end chair.

"My pleasure." Matt cleared his throat a couple of times and stacked a few of the boxes to make more room around the table.

Breanna stood and massaged her left leg. "It smells so good, Mollie. And your timing is perfect. My legs were going to sleep kneeling among all these boxes."

Mollie handed out holly-print tea napkins and passed around a plate of cookies and bread.

Matt snagged a couple of slices and several cookies. "Breanna said you don't put lights on the tree."

"All in keeping with the Victorian theme. But I'm not enough of a purist to clamp candles onto the branches. Too dangerous if you ask me. The tinsel reflects enough light from the room to make the tree glisten."

Breanna wrinkled her nose.

"I know. You're not fond of tinsel, so I'll make a concession this year." She leveled a look at Matt. "When you've finished with the tree, the two of you decide whether it needs the traditional tinsel." She raised a china cup and looked from Matt to Breanna, a smug expression seaming her lips.

"Oh, no." Matt raised a hand in protest and shook his head. "I'm not getting in the middle of this."

"Too late," Breanna teased. "You're already in."

An hour later, ornaments of every size and shape adorned the tree and Breanna stuffed the last few pieces of tissue into a carton.

Matt stacked several boxes and headed for the stairs.

She followed, balancing her own cardboard tower with a question. "So what do you think?"

"About?"

"Tinsel. What's your vote?"

He walked into the first bedroom at the top of the stairs and straight to the closet. "No tinsel."

Breanna smiled in victory and flipped the light switch with her elbow. She handed over her pile and inspected the room more closely while Matt stuffed away the boxes.

"Considering your wisdom on the tinsel, what's your honest opinion as a renovation expert?" She ran her hand over the smooth wood frame around the window. "Do you really think the trim in this room needs a paint job?"

She heard the closet door close, and when he made no reply, she turned to see him leaning against it with his arms folded.

She frowned. "What?"

"Can I ask you a personal question? Just say no if you're uncomfortable."

Uncomfortable? *Duh*—as her students said. What could he possibly want to know? She straightened her shoulders and raised her chin. "Ask away."

"Weren't you supposed to bring someone with you over the Christmas break? A boyfriend?"

At least he didn't beat around the bush. She stuck her hands in her jeans pockets and faced him squarely. "I was planning to talk to you about that tonight."

Pleasant surprise registered on his face.

"First of all, yes. My so-called boyfriend was supposed to come with me but he got tied up. With another woman."

Surprise amped up to shock, and he swept her with a quick appraisal. "You're kidding."

"No. I found them at the gym—*working out,* you might say."

"That's too bad," he said with not one speck of remorse.

"Not really." She lifted a shoulder. "I'd rather know now than later."

He pushed off the door and stood evenly on both feet. "So you're unattached?"

She considered his question and opted for humor. "You make it sound as if I'm rolling around, not yet bolted down."

He coughed out a laugh, rubbed a hand along the side of his head, and took a moment to regroup. "That's not exactly what I meant."

If she had one of Mollie's Victorian fans, she'd be whipping up a gale in front of her face at the moment. Instead, she pushed up her sleeves.

An easy smile lifted one side of his mouth. "What I should have said is, I've enjoyed your company these last couple of days, but I didn't want to tread where I wasn't welcome."

"Thank you." She looked at the floral wall paper, seeking emotional balance. "Me, too."

"So what were you going to mention to me?"

Exhaling her disgust in an audible breath, she refocused. "Aaron—the former boyfriend—and what's-her-name are coming here for the weekend."

Matt appeared as stunned as she was when she'd heard the news.

"I know. It's crazy. That's what was bothering Mollie this morning when we came back from the vet. A Tiffany Collins called and reserved two rooms for this Friday and Saturday, and Mollie didn't recognize the other party's name until after the call ended."

He wrapped a hand around the back of his neck. "Doesn't he know you're here?"

"According to Mollie, no. Their reservation is a surprise from Tiffany. Mollie offered to call back and say she had no rooms available, but I can't let her do that. She needs the money."

Breanna assessed the ruffled room. "This boarding house is her livelihood."

A soft whistle slipped through his teeth.

"Guess we'll have a full house this weekend." She braved a glance in his direction and caught him studying her. "Unless you move home."

He held her eyes for a moment. "What do *you* want?"

Startled by his straight-forward question, she deflected the missile. "It's not my decision."

Breanna held her breath, wanting to ask him to stay but determined not to. Like she'd said, not her call. But she couldn't just let it drop.

"Things are a little—" she motioned toward the curtains— "frilly around here. You strike me as more of a wood and leather type."

The dimple flashed. "Wood and leather, huh? You don't think I'm holding my own here?"

"That's not what I said."

"I'm not alone, you know."

She gave him a questioning look.

"I've got Roady."

Bemused, she walked to the door and laid her hand on the light switch. "Are you finished here?"

"Not really, but I think it's time to go."

His remark puzzled her even more. She flicked off the lights and left him in the dark. Trotting quickly down the stairs, she heard his heavier, slower footsteps behind her.

"Breanna."

The deep timbre of his voice stopped her. She tightened her grip on the handrail and held her breath as he stopped on the step above her.

A strong but gentle hand rested on her shoulder. "If Mollie wants the woodwork painted upstairs, don't you think we can do it for her?"

The "we" broke through her resolve. She exhaled a tight breath and faced him. His look held hers with a playful light, and she was helpless but to respond in kind. "You're right. We have three days before they get here. That should be plenty of time to fill the rooms with paint fumes."

He stepped down next to her on the narrow stairway and leaned close enough to brush her cheek with his breath. "Race you to the kitch-en for cider."

With that he reached around her to the railing and vaulted to the hallway.

Caught off guard by his daring, she dashed down the stairs after him. "You cheated!"

Laughing and taunting, they tussled into the kitchen like two children in bumper-cars.

Mollie stood before the stove, hands on hips. "And just what are you two doing making such a racket this time of night?" Merriment twinkled through a forced frown. "You're going to scare Roady out of his wits."

Breanna clamped a hand over her mouth and snickered. Matt peered through the glass into the back porch. "Some watch dog. He's sound asleep."

Chapter Eight

The next morning, Matt found Mollie at her post stirring pancake batter. Fresh coffee lured him to the counter. "You're amazing, Mollie, you know that?"

"Why, thank you, Matthew. Two pancakes or three?"

He groaned. "Two. I'm already fighting with my belt."

"They'll be ready in no time, but while you're waiting you can feed Roady. I haven't made it out there yet."

"Sure thing."

The dog greeted him with a whipping tail. Remarkable what the right food could do, not to mention a loving home. Matt filled the dog's dish with the prescribed amount and gave him a good rub all over. If he didn't know better, he'd swear Roady was smiling.

He checked the snowy backyard through the windows and noted a fence running around three sides. No dog house.

"He should start going outside." Matt closed the door to the porch and watched Roady work on breakfast."

"Is it warm enough?"

"Dogs are tougher than we think. He should be okay during the day."

Mollie flipped a golden disc. "Well, then, you can check the fence for me. I'm sure it has a few holes that need to be mended."

"I'll look around for a dog house, too, maybe throw something together from scrap out at my place."

Mollie set a plate of pancakes on the kitchen table and pointed at the butter and syrup. "Help yourself."

"You're spoiling me rotten. Cold cereal will never have the same appeal."

She poured herself a cup of coffee and joined him at the table. "You're going to think me a nosy old woman, Matthew, but I want to ask you a question."

He nodded as he buttered his breakfast. "How can I help?"

"Yesterday Breanna referred to Roady as 'Beast.' Is there something to that? Did he try to bite her?"

Matt laughed with a full mouth but managed not to spray the poor woman with pancake. "No, I think Roady may be harmless. Not much of a watchdog, at least not yet. And he didn't try to bite anyone—especially not Breanna. He adores her."

"And you know that how?"

"By the way he looks at her." He washed down the pancake with coffee. "It's written all over his face."

"Hmm." Mollie's eyes bored into him from above her teacup. "I see."

Sensing a hidden application behind her scrutiny, he resumed his pancake assault.

"So why 'Beast'?" she pressed.

He soaked up a small puddle of syrup with a forked bite. "Having Breanna and that dog in my truck yesterday made me think of the old fairytale about a beast and a beautiful woman. I laughed and Breanna asked, so I told her. I guess it stuck in her head."

Saying it out loud again made him feel stupid. Twenty-six-year-old bachelors didn't think about stuff like that. All the ruffles, lace, and tiny teacups must be fogging his brain.

Mollie took a sip of coffee and set the cup in its saucer. "That story has always been one of my favorites. It's very old, you know, much older than the animated movie version." She shifted her gaze to the window over the sink. "I like to think it's the story of God's love for us."

He hadn't seen that one coming. He sopped up another bite. Sermons didn't set well with breakfast no matter how you seasoned them.

But Mollie said nothing more. She took her cup to the sink, washed it out with a hand brush that held soap in the handle, and set it upside down on a towel to dry.

Edgy in the awkward silence, Matt finished his pancakes, downed his coffee, and took his dishes to the counter. "We're going to paint the woodwork upstairs for you. Do you have paint on hand, or do I need to get some?"

Mollie retied her apron sash, plumping the bow at her back. "You'll have to get a gallon. I think that will do, don't you? I saved an old can in the garage with the brand and number so they can mix the exact color for you down at the paint store." She looked at him good naturedly and patted his arm. "Tell them to put it on my account."

Relieved that she hadn't preached at him, he responded with a smile. "Will do. Anything else I can get for you in town? I'm going to run out to check on my place, and then I'll get the paint."

"Get brushes and whatever you need." She waved her hand as if dismissing him and returned to the stove. "All I have are tarps to cover the floors and furniture. Everything else belonged to the gentleman who painted last."

Mollie was a puzzle. She'd said just enough about that silly story to kick up his curiosity.

On his way down the hall he glanced at Breanna's closed door. Sleeping in or hiding? Last night's conversation upstairs had left him believing she was as much a puzzle as her grandmother. First the angry ex-girlfriend, then a blushing single woman, and finally a competitive rival. Which was she?

He grabbed his old coat off the hall tree and stepped into another brilliantly clear day. His breath clouded before him, and the dry snow squeaked beneath his boots as he crossed the lawn to his truck.

~

Relishing the comfort of her bed, Breanna tucked her knees up, slid one arm under her head and looked across the covers and out the bay window. Mountain peaks cut into the blue sky like shark's teeth, snowy white. Powdery mounds lay on pine trees in the yard, and the sun sparkled across them, flecking the branches with diamond dust.

She smelled pancakes and coffee. The muted baritone of Matt's voice from the kitchen had warmed her as much as the blankets. She'd listened contentedly as he visited with Mollie, his voice a low easy murmur. Before long, his heavy footsteps in the hall and the solid thud of the front door told her he was gone for the morning.

He'd taken the news of Aaron fairly well but turning the tables on her like that—asking what she wanted—had thrown her. To be honest, it frightened her. Yes, that was the emotion she'd not been able to identify. He scared her. Or rather, her growing fondness for him scared her. And in such a short time. What if he was another Aaron Reynolds? She couldn't do the roller-coaster thing again.

But Matt said he'd enjoyed her company. Said he didn't want to tread where he wasn't wanted. Oh, brother—if he only knew.

She tossed back the covers and dashed into the adjoining bathroom. An antique claw-foot tub sat against one wall with a wraparound shower curtain suspended from the ceiling. Plush throw rugs welcomed her bare feet and thick terry towels waited to embrace her face and body. Breanna began to fill the bath. The small stained-glass window and the mirror above the basin vanity clouded in the rising steam.

"Antique luxury." She twisted her hair into a clip and eased into the soothing water, sinking to cover her shoulders. Her grandmother's phrase had been the guideline along which they'd renovated the old house—the grace of a by-gone era with the conveniences of modern living. This little retreat was certainly a luxury when she thought of the basic bathroom in her Greeley apartment.

A knock came from the door leading into the hall.

"Good morning in there."

"I know, I'm late. I'll hurry." Breanna soaped a thick washcloth.

"No need, I'm running upstairs. Just wanted to say hello."

Mollie's footsteps tapped down the hall, daintier than Matt's a moment ago. Where did that woman get all her energy?

~

After breakfast, Breanna phoned in a "found dog" ad for the newspaper, vacuumed the rooms downstairs, took the trash out, and dust mopped the long hardwood hall and entryway. In a box upstairs, she found the faux pine garland and wrapped the open banister along the stairs, alternately inserting pinecones and deep red, silk poinsettias.

A second round of baking produced more small loaves, another glazed wreathe to freeze for later delivery, and several dozen cookies. At one point, she caught Mollie rubbing her knuckles after wrestling with the can opener. The woman would have to give in to electricity if she wanted to avoid the pain. Even in the comfort of the cozy home, Breanna knew the sharp winter cold bit into those aging joints.

Stomping feet on the entryway rug announced Matt's return. She opened her mouth but Mollie's voice chimed down the hall, "In the kitchen."

Matt appeared with a paint can in one hand and a plastic bag in the other, which he held aloft. "Brushes, masking tape, paint thinner, and dog biscuits for Roady."

"Oh, you dear," Mollie cooed. "You think of everything."

Breanna rolled her eyes.

"And in the bed of the truck, an igloo dog house. It's temporary, until I can build something better suited to the Victorian era."

Mollie reached up and patted his cheek with a flour-dusted hand. "Go give that beast a cookie."

Beast? Breanna eyed her grandmother.

"Yes, ma'am." Opening the box, he turned to Breanna. "You ready to paint?"

The white palm print on his face made her laugh outright. She untied her apron and used it to wipe flour from his cheek. "She got you, and you didn't even know it."

Standing so close to him sent flutters up her back. "I'm ready whenever you are." She grinned. Matt was so much fun to be around.

She hung the apron over a chair and took the sack from his hand. "I'll take these upstairs while you feed Roady. And while you're out there, grab the tarps. They're in the cupboard along the back wall below the windows." Feeling pushy, she added. "Please."

His eyes snapped with customary playfulness. "Yes, ma'am."

Anticipating the hovering heat upstairs mixed with the internal warmth that seemed to flare in Matt's presence, Breanna exchanged her bulky sweater for an old, long-sleeve T-shirt. She trotted up the stairs to the first bedroom on the right. Matt soon joined her with the paint and two tarps under his arms.

They scooted furniture away from the window and covered the floor with the spattered canvas.

"Paint or tape?" he said, holding the can in one hand and a roll of blue masking tape in the other.

"You're joking, right?" She took the roll and pulled off the shrink-wrapped plastic covering. "I don't even paint my nails."

He grabbed her hand and held it close, inspecting the tips of her fingers. "You're right. You don't." He dropped it with a grin, stooped to open the can, and stirred it with a flat stick.

Breanna pushed up her sleeves as Matt's cell phone went off.

Retrieving it from his pocket, he checked the caller ID and shot her a quick glance. "Be right back."

She didn't recall his phone ringing since she'd arrived. Who could it be? She had an ex—did he? Last night he hadn't acted like he had a girlfriend, but that didn't mean anything. Aaron obviously hadn't acted that way around Tiffany.

She ripped off a length of blue tape. *Lord, help me forgive Aaron. I need your help to do that. Help me let go of the hurt and anger—and him.*

When Matt returned, his expression revealed nothing about the caller.

"If we get a good system going, this should be quick work," he said, looking at the window. "I'm going to crack this a little for fresh air." He twisted the lock on top of the old sash frame and raised the window an inch. "With our low humidity, the paint should be dry by tomorrow or the next day."

Starting at the window, Breanna taped the edge of the floral-papered wall where it met the frame, and then the glass and metal catch and lock. A small stool helped her reach the top of the window.

Matt loaded his brush, and she moved to the closet. By the time she'd taped off the wall, doorknob plate, and hinges, he'd finished the window and started on the closet. She shifted to the hall door, and their "system" soon resulted in completion.

"We're a good team." The dimple flashed in a half smile.

Determined to take an emotional step forward, she looked directly at him. "We've had practice."

His smile spread. "A tree, a dog, and a paint can. Quite a history we've got."

They moved to the second bedroom across the landing and repeated the process. When they finished, Breanna began folding the surprisingly drip-free tarp. But Matt didn't take the paint downstairs, or even put the lid on the can.

"We can do the other bedroom, too."

His somber tone set off a warning bell.

"You don't want to sleep in a freshly-painted room that soon, do you?"

His expression confirmed her alarm. "I won't be. That phone call was the appliance store. My furnace is in, and I'm picking it up this afternoon. I hope to get it installed so I can try it out tonight."

She was staring at him, but she couldn't help it. Her heart suddenly weighed as much as the heavy canvas in her arms.

"Oh." She forced herself to look away. "Well, let's get finished then."

He took a step toward her, but she hurried out and into his room beyond the landing. The biggest room, it spanned the second floor and had a window in each of the three outside walls. His drafting table stood on the west end where the afternoon light served him best. Work boots waited beside the rocker at the foot of the brass bed, and a down vest and flannel plaid shirt hung over the foot board. Those few masculine items changed the tone of the room, added substance to the ruffled curtains and crocheted dresser scarf.

At the sound of his approach, she moved to the east window and spread out the tarp. Together they shifted furniture to the center of the room, but the comfortable camaraderie between them had vanished. Breanna chewed on the inside of her cheek to keep her emotions in check.

It shouldn't matter that he was leaving. But it did.

A new fear bubbled to the surface—fear that if he left, he wouldn't return. No more...what? Playfulness? Tenderness? Maleness in her completely womanly world?

They worked with the same efficiency as in the other rooms, and soon Breanna was folding the tarp again.

Matt placed his brush on top of the paint can, picked up one end of the canvas, and brought the corners together. "You're good at this." His voice deepened. "Maybe you could come out and help me when I start putting the finishing touches on my place."

His expression mirrored the intensity in his voice, and he took a step toward her as she held up her end of the tarp. Raising his section to meet hers, he wrapped strong fingers around her hands. She released her corners, but he didn't let go.

Sweeping her features with a thirsty look, he paused at her mouth and returned to her eyes. "It's better this way."

"What do you mean?" She swallowed hard against a knot in her throat.

"Better that I'm not around when Aaron gets here."

She refused to voice her feelings but was unable to look away.

He closed the space between them and dipped his head to meet her lips with his.

Releasing one hand, he slipped his arm around her and pulled her against him.

When he lifted his head, he brushed his lips against her forehead. "See what I mean?"

The huskiness of his voice ignited familiar sparks, and they joined the others already dancing in her stomach. She opened her eyes and tugged a whisper out of her throat. "What's that got to do with Aaron?"

The parenthesis deepened. "If I'm here, I might feed him to the beast."

Chapter Nine

att's remark about Aaron was not a joke. Even though it restored a lighter mood with Breanna, he'd like nothing more than to feed Aaron to the dog. The guy was not only blind for leaving her, but stupid for coming here. Matt didn't buy that story about a "surprise" visit to the boarding house.

He'd initially decided to stay on through Christmas, even if his furnace came in. The warmth and companionship of the last few days had been what he dreamed of as a boy—*family*. And the idea of family posed daunting opposition when it came to the overrated freedoms of bachelorhood. He wanted to make Breanna and her grandmother a permanent part of his life, but that would take time. And now he had even less of that fleeting commodity because Aaron's imminent arrival changed things. He couldn't be around when the guy showed up.

Matt cleaned Mollie's paint brushes, stored the paint and other supplies in the garage, and put the tarps in the cabinet. Roady bounded around the yard while Matt situated the doghouse and stuffed in the old blankets. He repaired a couple of broken slats in the picket fence and set the water bowl by the door. Taking a visual inventory of the place, a bitter taste filled his mouth at the thought of leaving.

Breanna had disappeared, and her absence ached like a wound. After today's kiss, he believed she sensed the charge of electricity that shot through his muscles every time she came near. If Mollie hadn't remained in the kitchen after the flour incident, he would have pulled Breanna into his arms right there.

He rubbed the back of his neck and watched Roady romp in the snow.

Maybe he needed a break from Breanna—a chance to cool down.

~

Mollie's chronic cheerfulness helped Matt say goodbye as she warned him not to be a stranger.

"You know where we are and what time dinner is." She gathered one corner of her apron and wrapped it around her hands.

Breanna stood next to the grandfather clock, the top of her head not reaching its golden face. Quietly polite, she folded her arms at her waist. Did she stand that way as her students headed out the door for home? He doubted it. He imagined her lightly tapping the tops of their heads, giving each one a quick hug and a homework reminder.

The corners of her mouth curved up, but he saw through the thin smile to the disappointment beneath it, and his chest tightened. He wanted to never disappoint her. He wanted to tell her that, and he hoped she read the promise in his eyes.

He hefted his duffle bag over his shoulder and opened the heavy oak door.

"Thank you for everything." He gave Mollie's shoulders a light hug.

"There's a candlelight service Christmas Eve at the church, Matthew." Mollie stepped into the open doorway as he walked out on the porch. "We'd love to see you there."

He grinned at her over his shoulder. "You never know, Mollie. I just might make an appearance."

"Good luck with your furnace." She raised her voice to carry across the snowy yard.

Maybe it won't work, and I'll be back tonight.

He slammed the truck door, started the engine, and cranked up the heater. Fastening his seatbelt, he glanced at the house. Mollie stood on the threshold wringing her hands in her apron. He didn't see Breanna anywhere.

Anywhere but in his heart as he pulled away from the curb.

~

Breanna felt the warm drop slip over her lower lashes and down her cheek. Mollie softly closed the door, and when she turned around her blue eyes shone with the same moisture.

"I know, dear. I miss him too."

She hid in her grandmother's embrace. "Why do men always make us cry?"

Mollie gently stroked her hair. "I suppose it's because we love them."

Breanna pulled back and saw a lifetime of wisdom in the little woman's face—creases at the corners of her loving eyes, laugh lines edging her prim, pink lips.

"Let's have a cup of tea and plan our deliveries." Mollie slipped an arm around Breanna's waist, and they headed to the kitchen.

~

Giving had always been the bigger part of Christmas at the Murphy home. On Wednesday morning, Breanna gathered baskets and boxes from the pantry and set them on the kitchen table. She spread several holly-printed napkins in the bottom of each one, and Mollie filled them with plastic-wrapped loaves and curly-ribboned cookie bundles. The two women loaded the back of Breanna's Jeep until it resembled Santa's sleigh, and they made their rounds to several shut-ins, the convalescent home, Mollie's favorite bank teller, and the pastor's family.

Several stops required a brief visit over tea or coffee and other homemade delights, and by the time they made it home, neither wanted dinner.

It's so quiet.

Breanna shuddered at the emptiness, the absence of heavy footfall and male laughter. Matt's laughter. She helped Mollie clean the kitchen and wondered if such quiet had prompted her grandmother to convert her home into a boarding house. She certainly couldn't blame her. Breanna had no siblings. And who knew how long it would be before she had a husband and children to share.

Shivering at a vision of Matt playing with a small, dark-haired boy with shining eyes, she went out the back door to call Roady. At her call, he eased out of the igloo opening of the doghouse and bounded across the yard. Even this rag-tag dog offered companionship. She hoped he wouldn't be too much for her grandmother to handle once she returned to school.

~

Friday afternoon Breanna tidied the entryway and bentwood coatrack, plumped pillows on the rose-colored damask settees in the parlor, and adjusted the thermostat. The temperature had dropped, and through the beveled glass oval in the front door, she saw the sky had darkened to a dull gray—sure sign of a coming storm.

Oh Lord, please don't let Aaron and Tiffany get snowed in here!

Determined to make herself scarce during Tiffany's and Aaron's stay, Breanna warned Mollie that she might not be sharing the evening meal with them. For Mollie's sake, she hoped Tiffany was enough of a conversationalist to get them through two dinners.

As if summoned, Aaron's SUV pulled into view and stopped in front of the house.

Breanna jumped back from the door like a mouse from a viper. Her heart kicked into high gear, and she scurried to the small side window to watch her replacement and former boyfriend approach.

Neither of them exited the car. Squinting, she caught what appeared to be animated conversation inside the vehicle. Finally the passenger door opened and out bounced the blonde from the gym, bundled in a bright purple parka and skin-tight leggings with white, furry, knee-high boots.

Breanna didn't know whether to gag or cry.

Tiffany stomped onto the porch and pushed the doorbell.

Mollie hurried down the hall fluttering her hands at Breanna. "Off with you, now. Let me handle this."

Breanna's cowardly attitude shamed her, and she held her post behind the coatrack.

Mollie smoothed her apron, tucked a strand of wispy white into her twisted topknot, and opened the door. "Hello. You must be Tiffany Collins. Do come in." She moved aside to make way for her guest.

Tiffany stormed through the door and flung her long hair over her shoulder with an impatient toss. "Mrs. Murphy?"

"Yes." Mollie looked over Tiffany's shoulder to the car parked out front. "Is everything all right?"

"No." She took in the entryway, the grandfather clock, and the coatrack.

Breanna stepped from behind it and raised her chin. "Hello."

Tiffany huffed out a breath. "The problem isn't with your place here, it's with *him*." She jerked a thumb over her shoulder. "He won't come in. Now I know why."

Breanna stood her ground and tried not to smirk.

"I know I can't get my online deposit back, but we won't be staying." She slid a look at Breanna as if sizing her up. "Thanks anyway."

With that, Tiffany spun on her furry foot and stomped down the stairs and across the yard. As soon as her door closed, the SUV jerked into the street and sped away.

Mollie shut the door and looked at Breanna. They both burst into laughter and giggled their way down the hall to the kitchen.

Mollie wiped her tearing eyes with a corner of her apron. "I think the good Lord took care of everything. Mr. Reynolds seems to have gotten exactly what he deserved."

~

The furnace worked perfectly, but Matt didn't experience the relief he'd expected. What once thrilled him as the prospect of creative renovation now threatened him with exile. An even heat circulated through the old ranch house, but the walls felt cold around him. No lilting laughter warmed his soul, no aromas emanated from his oven or simmered on his stovetop. No tree stood in his sprawling living room, and no Breanna curled up on his dark brown sofa.

"You seem like a wood and leather type." She'd pegged him. His overhaul efforts revealed hardwood flooring he'd found beneath outdated carpeting. Open beam construction covered the main living room and a dining area, and he'd attached a heavy mantel piece across the top of the stone fireplace that took up the entire east wall.

A big empty house for a big empty weekend.

His cell rang and his heart rate jerked up a notch. Caller ID revealed a fellow freelance architect. He let the call go to voicemail and laid the phone on the long counter that separated the kitchen from the dining area. At the refrigerator, he searched for catsup and found soured orange juice and a shriveled, two-week-old slice of pizza. The freezer offered little more—two frozen dinners and a boxed banana cream pie. What he wouldn't give for a loaf of warm pumpkin bread and the loving presence of the one who baked it.

Loving. There was a word that hadn't fit his vocabulary until lately. He'd fallen in love with Breanna Murphy, and he didn't mind admitting it. If that Aaron jerk did or said anything to hurt her this weekend, he'd …

He'd feed him to Roady a piece at a time.

A wicked grin curled his lip as he pulled out a frozen Salisbury steak meal and tossed it in the microwave. So much for home cooking.

~

Out of self-preservation, Matt drove into town Saturday afternoon for groceries and took the long way around past a certain boarding house. The pale yellow, gingerbread-trimmed establishment sat as far from his architectural leanings as possible, but the sight of it twisted his gut. Breanna's white Jeep occupied the driveway, but no other cars were parked out front. He slowed as he drove by and cranked his head around to see if Roady was in the backyard. He even missed that stupid dog.

A sudden idea surged through his mind, and he headed toward Main Street and the downtown stores.

Strings of white Christmas lights framed the doorways and windows of nearly every shop lining the street, and a hand painted sign in the window of the corner drug store promised gifts inside. He parked and walked in feeling out of place and obvious. He'd never shopped for anything like this before, but he had to start somewhere.

A tall thin clerk approached from the pharmacy counter at the rear of the store. "May I help you?"

Matt nodded. "I need Christmas tree ornaments and gifts for women. Any suggestions?"

"Follow me." The man led him past a display of poinsettias and around a corner to an alcove stuffed with decorations, wrapping paper, and more.

Matt quickly found what he wanted, paid the cashier, and drove to the market. With a lighter heart he filled a grocery cart with all the staples he could think of, including milk and eggs, bacon, ground coffee, a couple of steaks, and baking potatoes. He also tossed in knock-off versions of favorites from Mollie's—pancake mix and frozen sausage biscuits. And one of those soap-in-the-handle brushes.

In the pet food aisle, he picked out a large rawhide bone, a rope toy, and a real dog dish made of stainless steel with no flowers painted on the edge. Mollie's generosity had her four-legged guest eating out of a china bowl. At least Roady'd had enough manners not to break it.

By the time he made it home, he felt better. He stocked his cupboards and fridge, set the gifts out on the counter, and started a fire in the fireplace. In spite of the new furnace, a fire seemed friendlier, warmer.

"Don't be a stranger," Mollie had said. He'd love to show up at dinner, take a seat across from Breanna, and stare a hole through Aaron's forehead. Instead, he walked to his bedroom for his drafting table. He'd move it to the living room, crank up the radio for background music, and work on some plans that needed his attention. He flipped on the light and stood staring at the blank space against the outside wall. It took him a moment to remember, and the irony tugged at his mouth. He'd left the table at the boarding house. Good reason to drop by.

After a broiled steak and baked potato, Matt decided to stick to his earlier resolve and stay away while Mollie's weekend guests were there. In truth, he didn't trust himself, and he didn't need to do anything to make Breanna think he was some kind of animal. Some kind of...

That blasted story had been stuck in his brain ever since Mollie's cryptic remark about God's love. God wasn't even in it, only people—one of them more animal than human.

Is that how God sees us? The same as animals?

No, there must be a connection between Mollie's puzzling comment and Breanna's take on church.

What better place to go when you're hurting and need help?

Definitely his mother's approach, but little good it had done her.

The old resentment tried to resurrect, but he ignored it. Breanna was nothing like his mother. Neither was Mollie. What had they found at church that his mother hadn't?

He tried out his new soap-brush as he cleaned his dishes and discovered why Mollie used one. Much better than saving dirty dishes in the dishwasher until there were enough to justify running it.

~

Sunday morning lumbered in with swollen gray clouds banked against the mountains. Breanna pulled on a knit cap and gloves and ran out to start her car. She scanned the street for a silver Dodge pickup. *As if.* She sighed and her breath puffed out in a wispy cloud. Maybe he'd show up at church.

Hugging her arms, she trotted back to the porch and stomped the snow off her boots. "It's cold out there, Mollie," she called and shut the front door. "Colder than it looks. And I think it's going to snow again." She hung her cap on the hall tree and stuck her gloves in the pockets of her coat.

This morning's service signaled the end of the weekend. At last. Though better than she'd originally feared, the two days had dragged on forever without Matt. Had it been only a week since their trip to Red Feather Lakes to cut the tree?

"I'm almost ready," Mollie called from her room.

"No rush. I'm warming the car so a few more minutes won't hurt." Breanna strolled into the dining room and stood before the overloaded tree. Hardly a branch bore fewer than three ornaments, and as she scanned them, childhood memories crowded in from across the years. Her gaze rested at last on the blue-shirted lumberjack near the top, right next to the shimmering glass angel. On a whim she ran upstairs to the room at the end of the landing, as if hoping to see a man's plaid shirt draped over the brass footboard. Instead, her breath caught at the sight of the drafting table beneath the window, and a slow smile spread across her face.

He's coming back.

She hugged her arms again and twirled in the doorway.

"Ready." Mollie's cheerful voice sounded below. "Coming."

Her grandmother stood bundled by the front door, Bible in hand and a quizzical look on her face as Breanna trotted down.

"He's coming back." Breanna hugged her grandmother, pinning her arms to her side.

"Who is, dear?"

"Matt." She felt giddy, like one of her students at the Christmas party on the last day before break. "He left his drafting table upstairs in his room. He has to come back for it." She pulled on her parka and raised the fur-trimmed hood. "Maybe he'll come today."

Mollie's eyes twinkled. "My but aren't you happy for such a gloomy day."

"But tonight's Christmas Eve, and you invited him to the candlelight service. Remember?" Breanna zipped up, tugged on her gloves, and grabbed her keys and Bible from a small table. "If he's not there this morning, he's sure to be there tonight, don't you think?"

Mollie flattened her lips and shook her head. "We'll have to wait and see. You can't push a man toward God and expect him to stick." Pulling up her collar and scrunching her shoulders she opened the door. "Let's go or we'll be late and miss all the singing."

Chapter Ten

Breanna loved Christmas. The baking, the carols, the decorations—even the snow. She knew it all stemmed from the way she'd been raised, all the wonderful holiday traditions that Mollie had instilled in her. So unlike Matt's childhood. Maybe that's why he hadn't shown up at church.

That one single fact saddened her, in spite of the pine-scented warmth of the sanctuary, the pastor's inspiring message about giving, the children's brief skit depicting Christ's birth—and being home again with Mollie. How could one little thing like Matt's absence cast a shadow over an otherwise joyous occasion?

Did she love Matt? Not in the sense that she loved Christmas, but was she falling in love with him?

The soothing strains of "White Christmas" drifted out from Mollie's office computer. Breanna tried her best to cling to a Christmassy mood as she set the table for their main meal of the day, but Roady's scratch at the porch door drew her to the kitchen. He whined to be let out.

"Oh, Roady, I'm sorry. I forgot about you." She knelt and wrapped her arms around the dog and let him kiss her chin. "You old lovable thing, you." His scruffy tail beat the air in delight, and he bounded out as soon as she opened the door.

It didn't take much to make him happy. She watched him shovel his snout through the snow, run into his doggie igloo and out again, and trot around the fence line. A home, good food, and people to love on him were all he needed. He'd done nothing to deserve any of it, but he had them all.

"Thank you for giving me all these things too, Lord," she whispered. "Forgive me for being ungrateful and self-centered."

The doorbell chimed through the house, and Breanna closed the porch door and headed down the hall.

"I'll get it," she called on her way past Mollie's room. She tried to see through the glass oval, but the person stood to the side, hidden by the doorframe. Was that the bed of a silver pickup in the street? Her heartbeat took off in a flutter of hope, and she quickened her pace.

"I come bearing gifts." Matt stood before the open door—in one hand a shiny red gift bag brimming with green tissue paper, and in the other the most beautiful white poinsettia Breanna had ever seen.

From the threshold, she pushed up on her toes and hugged him. "You came back!"

Obviously startled by her impulsive welcome, he stood grinning like a schoolboy, and a little red-faced, she noted with satisfaction.

"Don't just stand there in the cold. Come in!"

"Oh, Matthew," Mollie said, hurrying down the hall. "Let me get a good look at you." She reached up to clasp his face in both hands and turned his head from side to side. "I thought so."

"What?" Bewilderment furrowed his brow.

"You've lost weight since you left. You haven't been eating well, have you?"

His deep, throaty laugh sent chills up Breanna's neck.

"We've missed you, young man. And you're just in time for lunch."

He held out the poinsettia. "This is for you, Mollie."

Her eyes sparkled with delight as she took the giant plant from his hand. "Oh, it's lovely, Matthew. Absolutely perfect for the table. How thoughtful you are." She bustled off toward the dining room.

Mollie's welcome allowed Breanna to regain her composure and a bit of decorum. Embarrassed by her girlish display, she lingered near the hall tree, hands in pockets, chin tucked in the thick cowl of a dark blue sweater.

"This is for you." Matt moved closer and held out the glittering bag.

"Thank you." She accepted the gift with a shy smile. "You returned for your drafting table, didn't you?" She nodded toward the hall tree. "And your coat. I picked it up yesterday."

Matt took the final step between them and cupped her face in his hands. "I returned to see if you missed me." A teasing smile set the dimple in place. "Can I interpret your welcome as an answer to my question?"

Breanna's reply started in the pit of her stomach and spread across her cheeks in the typical warm flush. She looked at the green tissue.

He covered her hands with his, pulled the bag down and kissed her lightly on the forehead. "No peeking. You have to wait for Christmas."

"That would be tonight. We always open our gifts on Christmas Eve. Right after the candlelight service." She peered into the bag and attempted a pout. "Mollie didn't have to wait."

He pulled her into his arms, lightly crushing the bag between them. "That's different and you know it."

~

Breanna's welcome exceeded anything Matt had dared hope for. His frugal expectations had hinged on Aaron not worming his way into her heart over the weekend. He wouldn't put it past the guy to fake the whole new-girlfriend angle and show up acting pathetic and lonely.

Evidently Breanna's heart was parasite free, and Matt hoped to make it his.

On their way down the hall, she ducked into the dining room, and he followed his nose to the kitchen. Cinnamon hovered in the air, just below the aroma of roast beef, and he rubbed the back of his hand across his mouth in case he was drooling.

"Coffee's fresh and so are the cinnamon rolls." Mollie, whisk in hand, stirred vigorously at the stove. "If you promise not to spoil your appetite, you can help yourself."

"You know me, Mollie. Matthew Appetite Dawson."

She laughed contentedly. "It's so nice to have your good humor back." Laying the whisk aside, she came over to him with a conspiratorial gleam in her blue eyes and lowered her voice. "Someone we both know has missed that good humor a heap." She tilted her snowy head toward the dining room where Breanna was filling drinking glasses from the water pitcher.

His pulse kicked up a beat as he searched the woman's merry face for truth. "Really?"

She returned to the stove and clicked off the burner. "If you ask me, it was the longest weekend of her life."

Anger cut to the front of a long line of emotions vying for dominance. "Was it that bad having them here?"

"Humph." Mollie opened the cupboard for a pewter gravy boat, set it on the counter, and proceeded to fill it from the heavy kettle.

"Let me do that." Matt took the kettle and carefully poured out the thick brown gravy. His mouth watered unmercifully.

"Didn't even come inside."

Shock kicked the anger out of line. "You mean he and the new girl didn't stay?"

Mollie picked up the corners of her apron and took hold of the gravy dish. "Tiffany came in—you should have seen her—and said they wouldn't be staying because Aaron refused." She harrumphed again. "Then they drove off like a bat out of—well, you know."

Matt shoved an entire cinnamon roll into his mouth to keep from shouting and poured himself a cup of coffee. He found it hard to chew with a cheesy grin splitting his face in two.

Breanna walked in and caught him at the counter with his mouth full.

"Mollie must be getting soft to let you at the cinnamon rolls before lunch." Her lips curved in a teasing smile that sent his pulse into overtime. Gray eyes shone clear and nearly blue above her sapphire sweater, and she stopped in front of him and laid a hand on his chest.

He curled his fingers around hers.

"As soon as you swallow, would you mind getting three plates out of the cupboard behind your head, please?"

He squeezed her hand, coughed, and tried not to choke, and her giggling sent him into spasms with the effort. He managed to hand her the plates, and she mouthed a silent "thank you."

Mollie filled a cloth-lined basket with fresh rolls. "Matthew, take the mashed potatoes and green beans. I'll bring the gravy and rolls, and Breanna can take the roast and fruit salad."

Picking up the serving bowls, he followed Mollie to the table. "Is this Christmas dinner?"

"Heaven's no. That's tomorrow. Turkey and all the fixings. I always like to have something special on Sundays, you know. This roast will serve us through the week for sandwiches."

She paused and captured him with a small frown. "I guess you don't know, do you? Last Sunday you were in the mountains cutting our lovely tree. And you didn't take a room here until the previous Monday."

He took his place at the table. A week since the tree? And another week of incredible home-cooked meals? How had two women turned his life upside down in such a short time? Or was that right side up?

Mollie reached for his hand and Breanna's, and he took both of theirs. Breanna's slender fingers entwined in his, and he caught a small grin flash across Mollie's mouth.

"Would you do the honors, Bre?"

Breanna bowed her head, and her hair fell in a dark curtain against her cheeks. She paused for a moment and then began in a near whisper. "Thank You, Lord, for this most wonderful time of year. For sending Your son, Jesus. For this house and this food, and for loving us as we are. Amen."

As we are.

Her quiet prayer stirred something deep in his gut, unsettling him with a possible answer to his unvoiced question.

When he opened his eyes, she was watching him with such warmth that he thought his heart might explode. She'd be gone in a week and now that he'd seen what a family could be, he wouldn't survive without her.

~

By five o'clock the wind had kicked up, and snow drifts stretched long icy arms across the lawn. Matt stood at the front door, watching through the oval glass. Christmas lights from neighboring houses dimmed and brightened in the whirling snow. He frowned as he thought of Mollie and Breanna attending the evening candlelight service at church.

He tried to talk Mollie out of it, but the woman was more insistent than usual.

"We've not missed the Christmas Eve service in, well, you don't need to know how many years. I've never missed it, that's all. And I don't intend to miss it now."

He appealed to Breanna for help, but she simply shook her head in resignation.

He tried again. "The snow's coming down hard and fast, Mollie. You might want to call it a night and stay home this year."

The little woman pulled her coat on, draped a long, crocheted scarf over her head and around her throat, and stood her ground. "We're going to the candlelight service tonight, Matthew. You can come with us or stay here and worry, but we're going."

He'd seen that determination before. Somewhere along I-25 with a dog on the shoulder. But this lost cause stood all of five feet in dark wool, pink muffler, and snow boots. He heaved a sigh and reached for his jacket and gloves. "Then we're going in my truck. It's four-wheel drive and has more clearance than Breanna's Jeep. Wait here."

Matt opened the door and a snowy blast gushed into the entryway. He yanked it closed behind him and pushed through the drifts, head down and collar up. From the looks of things, Santa would need help tonight.

He turned the heater on high and pulled into the drive behind the Jeep. No sense plowing through any more snow than necessary.

Against his better judgment, he escorted the two women from the porch to his pickup. He lifted Mollie onto the seat, helped Breanna in, and ran around to the driver's side. "Everybody buckle your seatbelts."

"We don't live in the country like you, Matthew," Mollie said, fastening the center belt across her lap. "The church is only a few blocks from here. Turn left at the corner."

Street lights helped little in the swirling snow, but he managed to find the intersection by turning into a blank space with no lights—hoping it wasn't an unlit house. Within a half mile he pulled up in front of a small, steepled church. Light spilled from stained-glass windows and a dark figure with shovel in hand made passing sweeps at the steps leading to double doors.

Matt helped his passengers out, escorted them inside, and then parked in the lot next to the church. It was surprisingly full, he noted, evidence that others, too, had braved the storm to keep a tradition.

Tradition. He had very few, if any. Last Christmas he'd spent pouring over plans for a school gymnasium he'd hoped to bid on. The Christmas before that he didn't remember. For the most part, his adult life had been one continuous blur of sameness—like the snow whirling around him in the dark. And Breanna Murphy and her grandmother were colorful lights in the night offering warmth and companionship and ... love?

An unfamiliar scene met him as he entered the sanctuary. Candles raised a steady golden flame from every level surface around the edge of the room and on the podium, and pine boughs filled window ledges and tables. The room radiated peace, and it seeped inside him and settled against his soul.

Mollie's white top knot marked their location, and he ducked into an open place at the end of the pew. Breanna's sweet voice lifted with others in a traditional carol, and she reached for his hand, entwining her fingers in his.

He recognized the song from his teen years when the youth leader made sure he was around to help with the tree and be part of the program.

With a twist in his gut he realized those few special times had planted something inside him, something that stirred and reawakened a promise of unconditional love.

At the close of the song, a middle-aged man stepped to the podium. "Thank you all for coming tonight. We considered cancelling due to the storm, but we knew that many of you would brave the weather, so we continued as planned. However, for safety's sake, the service will be brief so you can return to your warm homes and families."

Matt thought of his new furnace and cold house. Not exactly where he wanted to be tonight.

The pastor kept his word about brevity and soon asked everyone to stand for the closing prayer.

"Father, we thank You for sending Your Son as our light in a dark world. Thank You for loving us as we are, but not leaving us like you found us, and instead transforming us with that love. Go with each of us tonight and take us safely to our homes. In Jesus' name we ask. Amen."

The man's prayer pushed open the door in Matt's mind, and the unvoiced question flooded in. *How will I ever be good enough for God?* The youth leader had told him he never would be, and that was why God sent Jesus—to love him as he was.

Breanna had echoed those words in her prayer. God loves us as we are. Suddenly he understood Mollie's mysterious comment about beauty and the beast: "I like to think it's the story of God's love for us."

~

Breanna's concern had blown away with the gust of snow that swept in the opened door. Matt could have refused to take them out in the storm. He could have let them go alone in her car, but he didn't. Instead he consented to Mollie's stubborn, if not unwise, insistence that they attend the candlelight service. And he took it upon himself to keep them safe. His kindness and care spoke volumes to her. She didn't need months to know that he was everything she believed him to be.

If only he'd find his way back to the Lord.

You can't push a man at God and expect him to stick, Mollie had said, and Breanna knew the truth in her grandmother's words. The pull must come from within. Like it had with Jim at that candlelight service so long ago. The last one they attended as a family before he died.

She joined Mollie in the kitchen where roast-beef sandwiches were heaped atop a china platter and warm pumpkin pie cooled on the counter. She carried the food to the dining room and on her return paused at the porch door to watch Matt with Roady. He rubbed down the dog and wiped its paws clean with an old towel. They'd forgotten about him earlier, but the doghouse had kept him dry and safe.

Matt's face took a lavish licking from the happy mutt.

"Everything's ready," Mollie announced. "Tell Matt to come in and wash up. He's no doubt covered with dog slobber." She bustled off with a tray of hot cocoa and cups.

Matt came inside and washed his hands and rinsed his face at the sink.

Breanna held a towel and waited. When he turned toward her with water dripping from his hands and chin, she smiled and lifted the towel to his face, patting it dry.

Taking the towel from her hands, he pulled her into his arms and kissed her soundly.

She pressed into him, and her hands slipped over his shoulders. His mouth brushed her eyelids, her brow, her hair, and she knew she'd found her favorite place.

"Come on you two," Mollie called.

Breanna giggled at Matt's caught-in-the-cookie jar expression. "We're in trouble now." She took his hand and led him to the dining room.

The table was pushed to one side and three chairs sat near the tree where gifts peeked out from beneath the branches.

"We're not as formal on Christmas Eve." Mollie passed around the plates. "If you'd rather sit on the floor, feel free. I would, but it's too much trouble getting up again."

Matt and Breanna sat cross legged near the tree and Mollie pulled her chair closer. "Bre, please offer the—"

"Mollie?" Matt cleared his throat. "I'd like to pray this time if it's all right with you."

Unexpected joy welled up in Breanna and threatened to spill over.

Matt reached for her hand and Mollie's, bowed his head, and waited a moment. "It's been a long time, Lord, but thank You." He cleared his throat again and his voice came out thicker. "Thank You for this home and these women and Your love. For loving me as I am. Amen."

"So be it." Mollie's mouth twitched with emotion.

Breanna squeezed his hand before letting go. "Amen."

A sudden gust rattled the dining room windows and snow hit the panes with a fury. Already it piled on the sill like frosting on a cake.

"You may be stuck here, Matthew." Mollie handed him a teacup of cocoa and raised her eyebrows. "Did you plan to drive home tonight?"

He shook his head, caught again with his mouth full of food. "No," he managed. "In fact, I was hoping you'd ask me to stay." He slid an expectant glance at Breanna.

"You know you're welcome here, but even though you left your drafting table, you didn't leave any extra clothes."

He grinned and finished his sandwich before answering. "My duffle bag's in the truck. In case you ladies decided to let me stay."

His candor and their laughter warmed Breanna's heart. He could stay forever as far as she was concerned.

"Should we let Roady in for the gift exchange?"

Breanna's shock at her grandmother's question caused the woman to lift her chin in defense. "I saw a few things under the tree that he might like. And Matthew, he'll be your responsibility. Don't let him get out of hand."

Matt threw Breanna a doubtful look and shrugged. "I'll do my best." He stood and headed toward the kitchen.

Roady surprised everyone when he quietly padded in and lay at Mollie's feet.

"Humph." She patted the top of his scruffy head. "Guess he knows whose house he's in." She signaled Breanna with a wave of her hand. "Well, let's get started. I can't stay up all night you know. I've got a turkey to cook in the morning."

It wasn't hard to know where each gift belonged, and Breanna piled several next to Roady who immediately started gnawing on an oversized rawhide bone. Mollie beamed as she accepted a large ribbon-wrapped basket, and Matt took his with a look of surprise.

Breanna settled back with a box from Mollie and the red bag on her lap. "Okay, one at a time. You go first, Mollie."

The woman clucked sweetly as she pulled one gift after another from the deep wicker basket but gave Breanna a heartfelt look when she unwrapped a high-end electric can opener.

"It's not a very fancy gift, but I knew you wouldn't use it if I gave it to you any other way," Breanna said.

Her grandmother examined the pictures on the box. "I have to admit I'm glad you got it, Bre. My hands aren't what they once were, and lately they've bothered me quite a bit. Thank you, dear. You're always so thoughtful."

Breanna turned to Matt. "You're next."

He shifted his weight and stretched out one leg. Two boxes sat before him, and he reached for the taller one.

"That's from me," Mollie said as he tore away the paper to reveal a gourmet bag of ground coffee. "You can enjoy that when you're not here. It's what I serve my guests."

"Thank you, Mollie. You must have known you've got me hooked."

He set the bag aside and picked up the next gift. The parenthesis popped into place as he pulled at the paper. He quirked an eyebrow at the lid of a plain cardboard box, but puzzlement followed when he lifted out a large, hand-thrown pottery coffee mug.

Mollie's blue eyes twinkled, and she quickly answered his unspoken question.

"She had my permission, Matthew. We'll just have to keep it out of sight of the guests."

A deep laugh tumbled in his throat, and Breanna felt it run along the back of her neck.

Cradling the mug in his hands, he leaned slightly toward her. "Now it's your turn."

From the size and shape of the silver, paper-wrapped bundle, she guessed Mollie's gift before she pulled out two of the latest novels from her favorite authors. "Oh, Mollie. You always know."

"I know you need a break sometimes from those little rascals you teach, and reading is a wonderful way to get away when you can't get away."

Breanna's fingers tingled in expectation of her last gift. She drew green tissue from the sparkling red bag and her breath caught at what she saw. Carefully she lifted out a painted glass ornament— Beauty in a golden ball gown. One hand lay delicately in the massive paw of the Beast, the other against his cheek as she looked up at him.

Stunned by the significance of Matt's gift, she reached for his arm. "It's beautiful," she whispered.

"Oh, let me see!" Mollie stood and held out her hand. "Why, Matthew, you amaze me." Approval hovered around her eyes. She returned the ornament to Breanna and kissed her cheek. "I hope I can count on you two to clean up and put Roady out. I'm suddenly very tired, and I'm going to turn in."

She bent down and planted a peck on top of Matt's head. "This has been a wonderful evening. Goodnight, dears. See you tomorrow morning."

After Mollie closed her bedroom door, Breanna stood to hang the ornament as close as possible to the lumberjack. She shivered as Matt wrapped one arm around her waist from behind and with the other hand took the figure and suspended it near the lumberjack and angel. Then he gently turned her to face him.

"You once asked Roady a question that I'd like to think you meant for me."

She laid her hands on his chest, recalling her words in the cab of his pickup. "If I say I love you, will you become a handsome prince?"

"That's it." His eyes darkened, and he traced the line of her cheek with his thumb. "There's not much hope of me turning into a handsome prince, but would you settle for a happy husband?"

Joy pooled within her, and she wrapped her fingers around his and kissed the palm of his hand.

"I love you, Breanna Murphy. Will you marry me in June?"

"June?"

"Sooner?"

She laughed. "No, June will be perfect. Even if it is six months away."

Mollie's music had been cycling through the play list all evening, but Breanna suddenly caught the familiar line of a favorite song.

"Go tell it on the mountain ..." And that was exactly what she wanted to do—stand on the tallest mountain peak and tell the world she was finally at home in the arms of the man she loved.

~~~
~~~

Thank you for reading *A Mistletoe Christmas* and *A Boarding House Christmas*. If you enjoyed them, please leave a brief review on your favorite book retailer. It's the best Christmas gift you can give an author!

For my historical Christmas stories, try *The Snowbound Bride* or *Just In Time for Christmas* and *Snow Angel,* both combined in *High-Country Christmas Romance Collection*. You may also enjoy the Christmas theme in *Loving the Horseman,* Book 1 of "The Cañon City Chronicles." Links to each story as well as my other novels and novellas can be found at my website: www.davalynnspencer.com.

Receive a free historical novella when you join my quarterly newsletter!

~

May the Joy of Jesus fill your heart this season and may all that you read be uplifting.

www.davalynnspencer.com

About the Author

Internationally acclaimed novelist and Will Rogers Gold Medallion winner, Davalynn Spencer writes Western romance set along the Front Range of Colorado's Rocky Mountains. She is a Publisher's Weekly and ECPA bestselling author of both contemporary and historical fiction. An award-winning rodeo journalist and former crime-beat reporter, she also teaches writing workshops and plays on her church worship team. Connect with her at https://www.davalynnspencer.com.